STAR WARS
THE LIFE AND LEGEND OF
OBI-WAN KENOBI

BY RYDER WINDHAM

SCHOLASTIC INC.

New York Toronto London Auckland Sydney Mexico City New Delhi Hong Kong

www.starwars.com
www.scholastic.com

Library of Congress Cataloging-in-Publication data is available

ISBN-13: 978-0-545-08559-5
ISBN-10: 0-545-08559-4

12 11 10 9 8 7 6 5 4 3 2 1   8 9 10 11 12/0

Cover art by Hugh Fleming
Printed in China.
First printing, September 2008

For Frank Thorne, my favorite wizard,
and everyone who ever wanted a real lightsaber

ACKNOWLEDGMENTS

It would be impossible to compile the adventures of Obi-Wan Kenobi in a single volume, especially because many adventures have yet to be written. But for readers who hanker to read more about Obi-Wan, I highly recommend the *Star Wars* serial novels *Jedi Apprentice*, *Jedi Quest*, and *Last of the Jedi*, all written by Jude Watson.

While this novel introduces new details about Obi-Wan Kenobi, it also draws from various previously published *Star Wars* stories, including *The Star Wars Radio Dramatization* by Brian Daley; the novel *Star Wars: Shadows of the Empire* by Steve Perry; the novel *Star Wars: Dark Lord: The Rise of Darth Vader* by James Luceno; the comic book *Star Wars: Legacy #16* by John Ostrander and Jan Duursema; the comic book story "Luke Skywalker's Walkabout" by Phil Norwood; and the novel *Star Wars: Heir to the Empire* by Timothy Zahn. I am indebted to all these talented writers, as well as to the screenwriters of the *Star Wars* films: George Lucas, Lawrence Kasdan, Leigh Brackett, and Jonathan Hales. Enormous thanks also to Annmarie Nye at Scholastic, and to J.W. Rinzler and Leland Chee at Lucasfilm, for their collective support and always valued input.

STAR WARS

THE LIFE AND LEGEND OF
OBI-WAN KENOBI

PROLOGUE

Luke Skywalker was surprised to see the moisture vaporator standing beside Ben Kenobi's abandoned hut on Tatooine. Given that over three years had transpired since Ben left the desert planet, Luke had assumed the vaporator would be long gone, scavenged by the Jawas or Sand People. Incredibly, both the vaporator and Ben's hut appeared to be in good shape.

The sun-bleached dwelling hugged a remote, stony bluff in the Jundland Wastes with a sweeping view of the Western Dune Sea. Luke had landed his X-wing starfighter nearby, and was eager to get out from under Tatooine's blazing twin suns. But as he trudged across the rocky ground and drew closer to the plasteel door that was the entrance to Kenobi's hut, he sensed a strange tension in the air. It reminded him of the disturbing sensation he had felt on Dagobah, at the cave that was so strong with the dark side of the Force. But while that cave had radiated cold and death, and seemed to challenge and beckon Luke to enter, this was an entirely different feeling — as if the entire property were saying Go away.

However, Luke also sensed that the message was not for him. He wondered if Ben had used the Force to protect his home, and figured he'd find out soon enough.

The plasteel door was unlocked. Luke slid it open and stepped inside. The air was musty, but the shadowy interior offered at least some relief from the heat. Looking around at the various relics that rested on small tables and shelves, and the animal pelts stretched out on the semicircular couch that had also served as Ben's bed, Luke couldn't see that anything had been damaged or stolen. The only obvious evidence of Ben's absence was the thin dusting of sand that covered everything.

Luke moved down into the small living area, where he found a vacuum-seal chest on the floor beside a structural column. It was from this chest that Ben had extracted Luke's first lightsaber, the same lightsaber that Ben claimed had previously belonged to Luke's father.

Luke brushed the sand from the chest's lid, then lifted it and looked inside.

It was empty.

Luke sighed. He hadn't expected the chest to contain a second lightsaber, but he had hoped to find something useful. If not a datatape or holographic recording, at least some kind of clue that might answer the questions that had been gnawing at him for months, ever since his duel with Darth Vader on Cloud City.

As he thought of that devastating encounter, which had cost him not only his inherited weapon but his right hand, he suddenly felt an aching sensation at his wrist. Phantom limb pain, he recalled. That was the term that the medical droid had used to describe the occasional ache that Luke might feel from time to time.

Luke flexed the lifelike, mechanical fingers of the prosthetic hand that the droid had so carefully attached to the end of his right arm. Veins, muscles, and bones had been replaced with wires, pistons, and metal, and sensory impulse lines even made his cybernetic fingers touch-sensitive. Despite the fact that Luke's original right hand had been lost in the reactor shaft at Cloud City, the medical droid — an expert with highly specialized techniques of genetic reconstruction — had replicated a perfect synthetic duplicate, right down to the fingerprints.

But the medical droid couldn't do anything about the phantom pain. Luke would have to live with that.

He continued his inspection of Ben's home. It didn't take long to find the trapdoor in the floor that led to the cellar. A short series of steps, hewn from bedrock, descended into darkness. Luke pulled a small glowrod from his belt, activated its light, and climbed down the steps. The cellar wasn't entirely dark, as a scant, eerie light emanated from luminescent stone that was set in one wall.

Ben had used the cellar for food and water storage, and a small variety of dried fruits, vegetables, and meats — all of which now looked like collapsed bits of leather — remained strung to a metal pipe that traveled to a cistern. Luke also found a workbench that had been constructed from scrap metal. Tools were neatly arranged on shelves, but a few select tools rested on the workbench, as if waiting for their owner's return.

Then Luke spotted the box. It was an intricately carved boa-wood box, resting on the floor between the workbench and small auxiliary generator. Luke was moving the glowrod closer to the box when a sudden sound came from above.

Thud!

In a swift, fluid motion, Luke spun to his left as he reached fast for the blaster that was holstered at his right hip, and then sprang back toward the cellar steps. He brought his blaster up fast so that its barrel was angled up through the open trap door. An instant later, the air was filled by a panicked, electronic shriek.

The shriek came from the domed head of Luke's astromech droid, R2-D2, who had traveled with him and helped to evade the Imperial blockade around Tatooine. The startled droid unleashed a flurry of angry beeps as he peered down at Luke, then he stomped his treads at the edge of the trap door's opening, kicking up the layer of sand that rested on the floor of the upper room.

"Sorry, Artoo," Luke said as he lowered his blaster. "Guess I'm a little jumpy." As he returned his weapon to its holster, he muttered, "I'll probably stay that way until we find . . . Han."

Luke's throat was already dry from the desert heat, but as he said Han's name, he felt as if he might choke. He had no idea where his friend Han was, only that the armored bounty hunter Boba Fett had taken Han's carbonite-frozen body from Cloud City. Various reports confirmed that Boba Fett intended to deliver Han to the Tatooine-based gangster Jabba the Hutt, but so far, Boba Fett was a no-show. It was Luke's other friend, the Alliance leader Princess Leia Organa, who had instructed him to hide out on Tatooine and wait for some sign of Han.

Unfortunately, Luke had never been very good at waiting.

From above, R2-D2 emitted a series of soft electronic beeps and a short whistle. Recognizing the whistle's lilt as a concerned question from the droid, Luke replied, "I'm fine, Artoo. Go make sure the X-wing's camouflage net is secured, and I'll be up in a few minutes."

R2-D2 chirped a hesitant response, but then his motor whined and he backed away from the trapdoor.

The movement pushed some sand toward the trapdoor, sending it streaming down into the cellar. Luke shook his head. One way or another, sand found its way into just about every place on Tatooine.

While R2-D2 headed back outside to inspect the X-wing, Luke returned to the boa-wood box and crouched down in front of it. Examining the box more closely with the glowrod, he noticed a tight cluster of buttons, and realized that the box was a keypad safe.

Luke stared hard at the keypad. Ben had never mentioned this box in his basement, and Luke could only imagine what the access code might be. Struggling to recall whether Ben had ever hinted at the code, Luke thought back to that fateful day when Ben — in the room just above Luke's head — had revealed himself to be a Jedi Knight and told Luke about the Force. Luke seriously doubted that Ben would have programmed any obvious letter combination, like JEDI or THE FORCE. He wished he could somehow ask Ben himself, but after their last exchange, that seemed very unlikely.

Since Dagobah, Luke had been on his own.

For a moment, he considered breaking the box open, using a small prybar he had noticed on the workbench, but then he dismissed the idea. As much as he was curious about the box's contents, he didn't want to damage it. He reached cautiously toward the box, brushing the tips of his fingers against the keypad.

Snap!

Luke flinched and pulled his fingers back as the keypad automatically slid aside on an inlaid track to reveal a thumbprint clasp. He wasn't sure what had just happened, but somehow, he had bypassed the keypad. He hesitated for a moment, then thought, Here goes nothing. *He pressed his right thumb against the clasp.*

Clack!

The clasp yielded to his touch, and Luke saw a thin black slit appear along the lower edge of the box's lid. He lifted the lid slowly with one hand, adjusted the glowrod with the other, and peered inside the box. The first thing he saw was a flashpacket, an explosive device that had been affixed near the back of the keypad.

Luke eyed the flashpacket warily. It certainly appeared that Ben had rigged the box to explode, but for whatever reason, it hadn't worked. Luke thought, Maybe it's a dud. . . .

Another possibility suddenly struck him. Maybe Ben not only left this box behind for me, but also set it to explode if anyone else attempted to open it. But how? Did Ben somehow obtain my fingerprints? Did he foresee that I would lose my hand? Or was the clasp engineered to recognize me by the Force? *Luke was mystified, but if it turned out that his fingerprints had been all that prevented the flashpacket from detonating, he would have another reason to be grateful to the medical droid who had recreated his hand.*

Peering past the flashpacket, Luke saw that the box

contained some rectangular objects. He recognized them as books. Although he was far more familiar with datapads for information storage, he had seen enough books in his lifetime to know how what they were and how to use them. The largest book was a leather-bound volume that appeared quite ancient. Luke picked it up, and noticed that it too was sealed by a thumbclasp.

He pressed his right thumb against the clasp. The clasp yielded without a sound.

Luke wasn't surprised to find another flashpacket, this one affixed behind the book's front cover. Nor was he surprised that the explosive didn't detonate. What surprised him were the handwritten words on the book's first page.

> Luke,
> The flashpackets were a necessary precaution. I trust you will dispose of them properly.
> The future of the Jedi Knights is in your hands. Read these books and use them wisely.
> May the Force be with you.
> — Obi-Wan Kenobi

Luke blinked at the words as if to confirm they were real, that he wasn't just having a dream. The book felt suddenly heavy in his hands. He set it down carefully upon the workbench and, by the light of his glowrod, he began turning the pages. Every page was filled with handwritten text, and his heart began pounding harder as the various words and phrases caught his attention. Jedi Council . . . Old Republic . . . Battle of Naboo . . . Sith Lords . . . Jedi Temple . . . Separatist Movement . . . Battle of Geonosis . . . the Clone Wars . . .

Luke stopped to catch his breath. He knew he should start at the beginning, but the book was so thick, and he was impatient to find two names in particular. He began flipping through the pages even faster, scanning the text for the names — Anakin Skywalker *and* Darth Vader *— that he believed were the keys to the answers he sought.*

Ever since the duel on Cloud City, his thoughts had been dominated by two questions:

Is Darth Vader really my father?

And if he is, why didn't Ben tell me the truth?

The dull ache returned to Luke's right wrist, and he stopped turning pages. He hadn't found the names he was looking for, but had come to a section that contained Ben's instructions for the construction of lightsabers. The section included numerous illustrations by Ben himself.

Luke hadn't considered the possibility of building a lightsaber. Only after he lost his lightsaber at Cloud City did he realize that he had no idea where to obtain another one, let alone how to go about making one from scratch. Now, thanks to Ben's book, it seemed he might actually stand a good chance at replacing it.

9

A skilled Jedi can complete a basic light-saber in a few days if necessary, but creating one for the first time can take many months. The most essential component is the focusing crystal, preferably a natural jewel, which can be . . .

Luke was transfixed, nearly forgetting his intent to find information about his father's identity. He flipped back a few pages and began reading from the beginning of the entry.

Like most Jedi younglings, I constructed my first lightsaber at the Jedi Temple on Coruscant. Although it was merely a competent weapon, I would be a liar if I said I built it purely for training exercises. I crafted it with much thought and care, and dared to imagine that it would serve me well in the future.

In fact, I did use the weapon during my earliest missions with my Master, but it was not until . . .

Seeing the word Master, *Luke skimmed ahead. He suspected Ben was referring to Master Yoda, but he didn't see Yoda's name written anywhere. Luke went back to where he had left off.*

. . . but it was not until after we went to Ilum,

when I was still in my thirteenth year, that I learned the true power of a lightsaber.

Luke turned the page. He had expected the journal to provide details about what Kenobi had experienced in his thirteenth year that made him learn "the true power of a lightsaber," but as he read through the next few pages, it appeared that the elder Jedi may have kept that information to himself. Ben had also mentioned being "on Ilum," but there wasn't another mention of Ilum either, at least not that Luke could plainly see.

Luke frowned. Although he was eager to read the entire book, he also believed that building a new lightsaber might be his first priority. According to Ben's instructions, first-time efforts at lightsaber construction could "take months." Luke and his allies didn't know Han Solo's current whereabouts and had yet to formulate a rescue plan, but if they were going up against Boba Fett or Jabba the Hutt, Luke had a feeling that a lightsaber would be useful.

As Luke reexamined the instructions for lightsaber construction, his thoughts returned to Obi-Wan at age thirteen. What was he like then? *Luke wished he could have known more.*

CHAPTER ONE

Although the Jedi Order had deliberately banished Ilum from all standard star charts for many centuries, almost every Jedi trainee dreamed of visiting the sacred, secret planet in the Unknown Regions. That was because many generations of Jedi had gathered crystals from Ilum to energize their lightsabers, and some Jedi maintained that Ilum crystals were the finest in the galaxy.

Constructing a lightsaber on Ilum was not regarded as the most challenging trial for a Jedi apprentice, but to Obi-Wan, it was confirmation that he would become a Jedi Knight. And if anyone appreciated the opportunity to become a Jedi, it was Obi-Wan. Less than a year earlier, when he was still just a few weeks shy of his thirteenth birthday, he was nearly convinced that no Jedi Knight or Master would ever choose him as an apprentice.

But those days were behind him now. The Jedi Knight Qui-Gon Jinn, with some encouragement from

Master Yoda, had taken Obi-Wan as his Padawan. Granted, they had gotten off to a rough start, and it only became rougher when Obi-Wan temporarily renounced the Jedi Order to join the revolution on the planet Melida/Daan, a decision that he quickly came to regret. Qui-Gon had forgiven him and accepted his return, but there remained an uneasiness between them. Still, despite their disagreements and conflicts, a bond *had* developed, and both were confident this bond would grow stronger over time.

And so it was that Obi-Wan and his Master, traveling in a small transport ship on loan from the Galactic Senate, had made the pilgrimage to the snow-covered world of Ilum. As Obi-Wan meditated over the blue crystal he had just harvested from the frigid cavern, Qui-Gon stood a short distance away, watching.

Using the Force, Obi-Wan Kenobi maneuvered the components of his lightsaber so that they hovered in the air in front of him. The blue crystal rotated slowly, then drifted into place within the lightsaber's energy chamber. Focusing all his attention on the components, he sealed the compartment, and then adjusted a locking mechanism. The lightsaber's assembly was complete.

With his lightsaber still floating before him, Obi-Wan shifted his gaze to his Master. Like Obi-Wan, Qui-Gon was wearing an insulated robe to protect him from the cold. Qui-Gon's eyes were on the floating lightsaber, but Obi-Wan thought he detected something

14

distant in the man's expression, as if his thoughts were elsewhere.

Obi-Wan's lightsaber wavered slightly. Obi-Wan waited a few seconds, then said, "Are you not supposed to say a few words, Master?"

Qui-Gon's eyes flicked to Obi-Wan's. "Ah, yes," he said. Returning his gaze to the hovering lightsaber, he recited, *"The crystal is the heart of the blade. The heart is the crystal of the Jedi. The Jedi is the crystal of the Force. The Force is the blade of the heart. All are intertwined: the crystal, the blade, the Jedi. You . . . are one."*

Obi-Wan heard Qui-Gon's hesitation in the final sentence, and thought he detected a hint of sorrow or regret in his Master's voice. As he reached out to grasp the floating lightsaber and lower it to his side, he said, "Have I done something wrong, Master?"

"No, Padawan," Qui-Gon answered. "You've done well. I regret it is I, for a change, who is not being mindful of the moment." Then Qui-Gon looked away, letting his gaze sweep over the cavern's interior. "It is unfortunate that such wondrous surroundings could become diminished by foolish memories."

Obi-Wan shook his head. "I am sorry, Master, but I don't understand."

Qui-Gon returned his gaze to Obi-Wan and said, "The last time I stood in this chamber, it was with Xanatos."

Obi-Wan swallowed hard. Xanatos had been Qui-Gon's previous Jedi apprentice. Strong with the Force and a brave warrior, Xanatos had served alongside Qui-Gon on numerous missions, but ultimately left the Jedi Order to ally with his biological father, a corrupt governor who had initiated a civil war on their homeworld, Telos IV. Qui-Gon had been forced to kill Xanatos's father, an act that did nothing to stop or divert Xanatos on his path to the dark side.

For years afterward, Qui-Gon had maintained that he might never take another apprentice, and that he eventually did was much to Obi-Wan's credit. But shortly after Obi-Wan became Qui-Gon's Padawan, Xanatos reemerged, seeking revenge against his former Master — and nearly destroying the Jedi Temple in the process. Obi-Wan had been with Qui-Gon when they caught up with Xanatos on Telos IV, and neither was able to stop the dark, former Jedi from deliberately ending his own life by plunging into a boiling black pool of acid.

"Xanatos wasn't your fault," Obi-Wan blurted out without thinking. Qui-Gon had not asked for his opinion, and he felt his face flush.

"Perhaps you're right," Qui-Gon replied. "But for a time, Xanatos *was* my responsibility. And he was also my friend."

Obi-Wan had no response for this. He had come to regard Xanatos as an embodiment of evil, and had a hard time believing that he could have ever been a friend to anyone.

Obi-Wan also felt a bit stung. The trip to Ilum was important to him, and he hadn't expected his Master's thoughts to dwell on Xanatos. He almost wished that Qui-Gon's memory of the failed apprentice had dissolved along with Xanatos himself on Telos IV, but he immediately buried the thought and banished it from his mind. Such a line of thinking could only lead to the dark side — Obi-Wan didn't need Master Yoda, Qui-Gon, or anyone else to remind him of that.

Qui-Gon sighed. "You have worked very hard toward this day, and I regret I allowed unpleasant memories to intrude. Forgive me, Obi-Wan."

Obi-Wan was taken aback by his Master's request for forgiveness. Although he wasn't sure whether to speak, he said, "I . . . I forgive you, Master."

"Then all is well," Qui-Gon said, smiling as he placed his broad hand on Obi-Wan's shoulder. "Come now, let us see the result of your handiwork, this blade you have created by the will of the Force."

Stepping back from Qui-Gon, Obi-Wan held his lightsaber out in front of him and thumbed the activation switch. The beam ignited, and the cavern's crystal-lined walls reflected its brilliant blue light as they magnified the sound of the weapon's distinctive hum.

Obi-Wan had been raised at the Jedi Temple and had more experience with lightsabers than many

Padawans his age. Still, his eyes went wide with surprise as he beheld the brilliant beam that extended before him. He had expected that the Ilum crystal would produce a more intense beam than the weapon's previous crystal, which he had selected from a supply at the Jedi Temple's lightsaber crafting facility. But he was not prepared for the way the Ilum crystal would make the weapon feel in his grasp.

It was different somehow. He tested it, sweeping the blade through the air. The blade was still pure energy and without weight, but it seemed more precise and focused.

Obi-Wan looked to Qui-Gon, who smiled as if he could read his Padawan's thoughts. Qui-Gon said, "Some Jedi claim that Ilum crystals make one feel more connected with the Force."

Before Obi-Wan could comment, a beeping sound came from the comlink at Qui-Gon's belt. Obi-Wan deactivated his lightsaber as Qui-Gon removed the comlink, listened briefly, and then said into it, "On our way."

"What is it, Master?"

"A mission," Qui-Gon said, returning the comlink to his belt. "We're to go to Ord Sigatt."

"Ord Sigatt?" Obi-Wan shook his head. "I've never heard of it."

"It's in the Outer Rim Territories."

Obi-Wan lifted his eyebrows. It wasn't every day that Jedi were assigned to the Outer Rim. He said, "Isn't that a little out of our usual jurisdiction?"

"Not when a Republic refinery ship and its crew goes missing there."

Qui-Gon turned and headed for the mouth of the cave. Obi-Wan clipped his lightsaber to his belt as he followed, walking fast to keep up with his Master's long strides. They returned to their transport, set the coordinates for Ord Sigatt into the navicomputer, and lifted away from the frozen world. Minutes later, they were racing through hyperspace to the Outer Rim.

Twelve thousand years before Obi-Wan's lifetime, when the Galactic Republic was attempting to expand its government beyond the more traveled trade routes, the Republic established advance military and scout bases on several remote worlds. These planets and moons were designated as *Ords*, an abbreviation of Ordnance/Regional Depots. Over time, the Jedi Order replaced the Republic milita, and some of the Ords evolved into weapons disposal centers and storage facilities, while others were adopted by colonists.

Ord Sigatt was a small, rocky planet with mostly barren terrain and a few scattered lakes. For centuries, its modest population consisted of people who stayed only until they found somewhere else to go. Some long-time colonists lived on the outskirts of the main settlement, but most lived close to the spaceport, the energy station, or the water treatment facility that made up the main settlement. As for tourism, most travelers regarded Ord Sigatt as little more than a place to rest or refuel their ships. But all that changed after a prospector's recent discovery of a large deposit of carvanium, a metal used in alloys such as durasteel.

Almost overnight, Ord Sigatt was transformed into a mining world. Many colonists became instantly wealthy when they sold their properties to offworld consortiums. Mammoth vehicles were delivered to excavate the carvanium, and the spaceport expanded to accommodate the refinery ships. The settlement's population increased rapidly with migrant laborers and soldiers of fortune, and a sprawl of temporary housing had sprung up for the new arrivals.

Obi-Wan reviewed these details during his journey with his Master through hyperspace, the time-space dimension that allowed for faster-than-lightspeed travel between planets. Studying transmitted data from the Jedi Temple, Obi-Wan said, "The missing refinery ship was the *Hardy Harrow* from Denon, and is owned by Denon-Ardru Mutual. The ship had been scheduled to pick up a shipment of carvanium two days ago, but when it failed to return to Republic space, a Denon Senator notified the Council."

"Any comment from Ord Sigatt Spaceport?" Qui-Gon asked.

"They say the *Hardy Harrow* never reached Ord Sigatt."

"What about recent acts of piracy or space weather anomalies in the system? Has anything been reported?"

"No, Master." A signal light flashed on the transport's console and Obi-Wan looked to a sensor screen. "We're coming out of hyperspace."

There was a slight shudder as the transport dropped out of hyperspace and entered realspace. Outside the transport's cockpit transparisteel window, a rush of bright light washed away from view and was replaced by a solitary planet amidst a field of distant stars. Obi-Wan confirmed that the planet was Ord Sigatt, then said, "I'll notify the spaceport that we'll be arriving in —"

"Easy, now, Padawan," Qui-Gon interrupted. "For all we know, the spaceport authorities may have something to do with the missing refinery. Let us arrive unannounced. We'll land in one of the public hangars on the outskirts."

After gaining clearance from the spaceport, they landed their transport in an open-roof hangar. Obi-Wan was somewhat relieved to learn that Ord Sigatt's climate was considerably warmer than Ilum, but as they stepped down the transport's landing ramp, he realized the air was not nearly so clean.

A starship maintenance droid directed them to the

hangar's exit. They had almost reached the exit when two uniformed security guards stepped out from the shadows to block their path. Both guards had blaster rifles slung over their shoulders, and their hard expressions indicated that they were prepared to use the weapons if necessary. One of the guards looked at Qui-Gon and snarled, "Either of you carrying weapons?"

Qui-Gon raised his right hand slowly and made a slight sweeping gesture with his fingers as he said, "We don't have any weapons."

Both guards were unaware that Qui-Gon was using the Force to manipulate their minds. The guard who had addressed Qui-Gon nodded and said, "No, you don't have any weapons."

"We're just harmless traders," Qui-Gon added. "You can let us go on our way."

"Totally harmless," the guard answered. "Go on, then." He and his partner stepped aside, allowing the two Jedi to move through the exit.

They stepped out onto a busy street, filled with pedestrian traffic and lined with merchant stalls. They walked past the stalls, keeping their lightsabers concealed within their robes. As they moved along, Qui-Gon leaned close to Obi-Wan and said in a low voice, "Notice anything unusual about the locals?"

Obi-Wan surveyed the area. He saw a mix of humans and aliens from various worlds, and most wore work clothes and coveralls. Some were seated at tables with food set out in the shade of a nearby hangar. All of the merchants seemed very focused on their customers.

Obi-Wan shrugged. "Well," he said, "it doesn't seem much different from any other spaceport on a backwater world. Except that people around here look glummer than most." It was true. No one appeared to be very happy about being on Ord Sigatt.

Qui-Gon said, "There's also the fact that no one is carrying any weapons."

As Obi-Wan's eyes flicked from one person to the next, he quickly confirmed his Master's observation. Except for the security guards that they'd left behind in the hangar, not a single being was wearing a holster or bearing weapons of any kind.

"That *is* unusual," Obi-Wan said. "Nothing in the report from the Jedi Council mentioned that blasters were prohibited. Maybe it's just the way the locals maintain peace."

"Maybe," Qui-Gon said, but Obi-Wan could tell that his Master was skeptical.

A trio of spacers walked by, and the Jedi watched the men enter a nearby bar, one of the older-looking buildings on the block. Qui-Gon said, "I might be able to pick up some information in there. You wait outside. I'll be back in a few minutes."

A few seconds after Qui-Gon entered the old building, Obi-Wan heard a loud crash. It had sounded from the alley right around the corner, which ran perpendicular to the main street. After a quick glance back toward the door of the bar, he walked around the corner and found himself looking at a burly Besalisk. The four-armed alien wore a stained apron and held two trays in his lower hands. A clutter of empty bottles lay scattered around his wide feet. It appeared he had just accidentally dropped the bottles.

Obi-Wan was about to turn back when the Besalisk, grumbling to himself, stooped down and began loading the bottles onto the trays with his upper arms. Obi-Wan was amazed at how fast the alien's hands moved. The Besalisk was reaching toward the last cup when he looked up at Obi-Wan. Eyes wide with surprise, the alien said, "Aw, nuts." Then he lowered the trays to the ground, raised all four of his meaty, four-fingered hands in the air and said, "I surrender."

Confused, Obi-Wan said, "You do?"

"I know better than to mess with Jedi," the Besalisk said, his bristly whiskers trembling slightly. "Even youngsters like yourself."

Suddenly self-concious, Obi-Wan glanced down to make sure his lightsaber had not accidentally become exposed. Seeing that it was still concealed beneath his robes, he returned his gaze to the Besalisk and said, "Who told you I was a Jedi?"

Arms still raised, the Beslisk chuckled, "*You* did, son. For one thing, you've got a Jedi apprentice's braid dangling down your shoulder. Also, maybe you don't know this, the weave of Jedi robes is pretty distinctive. The real giveaway was when you looked to your hip to make sure your lightsaber wasn't showing. Anyway, you caught Dexter Jettster fair and square."

Obi-Wan was astonished by the Besalisk's powers of observation. Taking a step into the alley, he kept his expression neutral as he said cautiously, "So . . . Dexter Jettster . . . you must *also* know why I'm here."

"Gotta hand it to you," Jettster said, winking at Obi-Wan. "I knew I couldn't keep running blasters out of my bar forever. I just never imagined Jedi would come after me."

Running blasters? Obi-Wan was baffled by Jettster's admission.

The Besalisk continued, "I won't beg for mercy. I know I done wrong. But I swear, Denon-Ardru Mutual and their security goons are the real troublemakers. Bad enough they take over the local government and confiscate everyone's weapons in the name of *their* law, but when they go stealing land from colonists here, well, I just had to do *something*. You'll find all the blasters in the back room of the bar. Hadn't begun distributing them to my friends yet."

As he listened, Obi-Wan's nimble mind began sifting through the information, connecting details that he already knew. He said, "Where is the *Hardy Harrow*?"

"Hidden in a valley, about twenty kilometers north of here," Jettster said. "It's not damaged. My friends and I here, we captured the ship shortly after it arrived in orbit and removed its transponder. We just wanted Denon-Ardru to know that we weren't going to leave Ord Sigatt without a fight."

"Did you harm the crew?"

"The *crew*?" Jettster wrinkled his brow at this, then said, "Come on, you know as well as I do that the *Harrow* is a drone barge, doesn't have a crew except for the droids that . . . that . . ." Jettster gasped, then he narrowed his gaze at Obi-Wan.

"Go on," Obi-Wan said.

Jettster shook his thick head. "Son of a gundark," he said. "You got me, Jedi. You tried to hide it, but I can see it in your eyes right now. You had no idea that I was up to anything but dropping bottles before I opened my big mouth. Until one minute ago, I prided myself on how well I kept secrets, but now —"

"*Help!*"

The cry — it sounded like a child's voice — came from outside the alley, behind Obi-Wan. He turned his head fast to see three security guards, carrying blaster rifles and clad in the same uniforms as the pair who'd stopped him and Qui-Gon at the hangar. One of the guards was gripping the collar of a young boy, who looked about nine years old. A younger child, a girl, clutched at the boy protectively.

Obi-Wan shot a severe glance at Jettster and said, "Stay here!" Then he ran out of the alley, where pedestrians had already formed a small crowd around the guards and the two children.

The guard who had grabbed at the boy growled, "I saw you throw that rock at me, whelp! Now you're going to pay for it!"

"Unhand him," Obi-Wan said as he moved toward the guards.

Keeping one hand on the boy's collar, the guard glanced at Obi-Wan and barked, "Back off, kid!" And then he shifted his blaster rifle, bringing it up toward Obi-Wan.

Obi-Wan's lightsaber flashed, sweeping through the rifle's barrel. The guard released the boy, who fell back into his young sister's arms as the shattered barrel fell and rolled across the street. The other two guards moved as if they were about to raise their own rifles, but then they looked beyond the blazing lightsaber to meet Obi-Wan's gaze.

"A Jedi," murmered a voice from the crowd. "He's a Jedi!"

A silence fell over the street, all eyes on Obi-Wan and the guards. Obi-Wan was about to order the guards to drop their weapons, but before he could get a word out, the entire crowd broke out in an exultant cheer.

Obi-Wan kept his eyes trained on the guards. As the crowd continued to cheer for the Jedi, the guards dropped their weapons. While the unarmed guards shifted nervously in the middle of the street, Obi-Wan felt a finger gently tapping at his right shoulder. He turned to see Qui-Gon standing behind him, and quickly deactivated his lightsaber.

Raising his voice so he could be heard over the applauding crowd, Qui-Gon said, "Should I have reminded you to stay out of trouble?"

Obi-Wan retorted, "*You* asked me to wait outside!" Remembering Dexter Jettster, he glanced back to the alley, where he saw Jettster leaning against the wall outside the bar. Jettster had joined in the applause, clapping hands with his two upper arms while using his lower hands to point to the ground. Jettster had stayed where he was told.

Obi-Wan thought, *He's really not a bad guy. Quite helpful, actually.*

Returning his gaze to his Master, Obi-Wan said, "Before you issue reprimands, shall I tell you where we'll find the *Hardy Harrow*?"

Qui-Gon stared at Obi-Wan for a moment, then said, "And just how did you come by this information?"

"A little four-winged bird told me."

Denon-Ardru Mutual had sent a small army of security guards to Ord-Sigatt, but all of the guards surrendered without protest to the Jedi. After all, they had been paid only to push *ordinary* people around. The guards returned to Denon in the *Hardy Harrow*, but without the carvanium shipment.

Neither the Galactic Senate nor the Jedi Council was pleased by a Denon Senator's attempt to use the Jedi to recover an unmanned drone barge, especially when they discovered the same Senator had a controlling interest in maintaining Denon-Ardru Mutual's secret monopoly on the carvanium from Ord Sigatt.

Obi-Wan and Qui-Gon remained on Ord-Sigatt for a few days to help return the local government to normal. They spent a good deal of time with Dexter Jettster, who not only impressed them with his keen observational skills and memory, but with his excellent cooking. It was during one meal that Jettster faced Obi-Wan and said, "Do you know the true power of a lightsaber?"

"The *true* power?" Obi-Wan echoed. He looked to Qui-Gon for support.

Qui-Gon said, "It's a fair question."

Returning his gaze to Jettster, Obi-Wan said, "Well, I suppose it's the lightsaber's ability to cut through almost anything."

Dexter beamed. "That's what I *used* to think," he said as he pushed another plate of food toward Qui-Gon. "But then one day, I saw a young Jedi named Obi-Wan Kenobi activate his lightsaber on Ord Sigatt. And that was when I learned the weapon's true power."

Obi-Wan shifted in his chair at the dining table. "I . . . I'm afraid I don't understand."

"Cutting through things is merely a lightsaber's technical function," Jettster continued. "But its real power is in the eye of the beholder. The sight of a light-saber can inspire great fear, but it can also inspire great hope. It all depends on whether one regards the Jedi as friend or foe." Reaching out with his right upper arm, Jettster placed his hand on Obi-Wan's shoulder and said, "With one quick sweep of a lightsaber, you gave hope to everyone who saw your blade. Except for the bad guys, that is. Your lightsaber brought *them* to their knees, and without spilling a drop of blood."

"Well," Obi-Wan said, "I *did* destroy the one guard's blaster —"

"Haw!" Dexter laughed. "That you did, but still . . . consider this, my young friend. Many weapons can kill, but only the lightsaber can inspire such extremes of hope or fear. And I shall add that I will be forever glad that only Jedi carry lightsabers." He raised his glass to Qui-Gon.

As the Jedi prepared to leave Ord-Sigatt, Jettster walked with them back to their waiting transport. As they neared the hangar, Jettster pulled Obi-Wan aside and whispered, "Listen, son. Thanks for not telling any-one how I blabbed about the blasters or the missing freighter. You saved my reputation."

Obi-Wan grinned. "Take care of yourself, Dexter," he said, extending his hand.

"A handshake just won't do, son," Dexter said, and he grabbed the boy and lifted him off his feet to embrace him in a four-armed hug. "Until we meet again."

INTERLUDE

With Ben Kenobi's journal spread open before him, Luke Skywalker reviewed the instructions for building lightsabers. Ben's cellar workshop was equipped with most of the tools he would need, but he would have to collect most of the weapon's electronic and mechanical parts from dealers, which meant a trip to one of Tatooine's spaceports. Mos Espa was closer to Ben's house, but was also crawling with Imperial spies, so he would have to go to Mos Eisley. Princess Leia, Han Solo's first mate Chewbacca the Wookiee, and their new ally Lando Calrissian were already in Mos Eisley, trying to gain information about the whereabouts of Boba Fett. Luke was expecting his friends to arrive soon and give him an update, so he could then ride back with them to Mos Eisley.

As for the lightsaber's focusing crystal, that would be the real trick. Because he didn't have any natural jewels at his disposal, he would need to build or buy a small furnace to create and form the jewel, and then he would have to cut the jewel and polish it. There was also the matter of installing the crystal and tuning the lightsaber's photoharmonics. Although Ben's instructions were clearly written, it seemed the entire construction process was an inexact science, and possibly dangerous. If Luke made even a minor error, the lightsaber could explode in his hands.

Luke was sitting at the low round table in Ben's living area as he prepared a list of components he hoped to obtain in Mos Eisley. Lifting his gaze, Luke saw R2-D2 standing on the other side of the table, watching him. It had been in this same room that Ben had first told Luke about how his father had been a Jedi Knight, who was betrayed and murdered by Ben's pupil, Darth Vader. Recalling Vader's contradictory claim at Cloud City, Luke wished he knew the whole story.

Ben had described Luke's father as a cunning warrior and a good friend. On Dagobah, Master Yoda had commented that Luke, like his father, had "much anger" in him. Were they even talking about the same person?

Luke wanted to read more of Ben's journal, but then he heard a landspeeder approach. He peered out a window to confirm the speeder carried Leia and the others. He quickly returned Ben's journal to the boa-wood box in the cellar, then instructed R2-D2 to stand guard while he went to Mos Eisley. As he left Ben's house, he found himself wondering absently, I wonder what my father was like when Ben first met him?

CHAPTER TWO

Qui-Gon should have returned by now, thought Obi-Wan Kenobi. He sat in the bridge of the gleaming Naboo Royal Starship, which had landed at the outskirts of Mos Espa Spaceport on the remote planet Tatooine. Obi-Wan was now twenty-five years old, and in his twelve years as Qui-Gon Jinn's apprentice, he had come to know his Master's eccentricities well.

Although Qui-Gon was regarded as a most capable Jedi Knight, he also had a reputation for ignoring rules and following his own instincts. He routinely questioned authority, including the Jedi Council. He had even turned down at least one opportunity to join the Council because he refused to be tied down to their "orthodox philosophies." He had excellent manners but seemed to prefer food that did not require utensils. He was almost overwhelmingly empathetic with all life forms, even if the creature happened to be some monster that was trying to take his head off.

But Obi-Wan had never known Qui-Gon to behave quite so irrationally as he had over the past two days. Looking out the bridge's viewport and seeing no sign of Qui-Gon on the surrounding desert wastes, he thought, *What's taking him so long?*

Qui-Gon and Obi-Wan were acting as emergency guardians for Queen Amidala of Naboo. Their original mission had been to dispel the Neimoidian Trade Federation's illegal blockade of Naboo, but that was before the Trade Federation's droids destroyed their Republic cruiser and tried to kill them. Hoping to deliver Amidala to Coruscant, where she could formally protest the Trade Federation's actions, the Jedi had fled Naboo with the Queen's entourage in the Royal Starship, only to be immediately attacked by Trade Federation forces. Had it not been for the swift action of the astromech droid R2-D2, who managed to repair the ship's damaged shield generator while under heavy fire, they never would have survived the escape. Unfortunately, the starship's T-14 hyperdrive was damaged beyond repair, leaving them unable to continue to Coruscant.

Seeking a safe place to land, Obi-Wan had used the ship's navicomputer to locate Tatooine, a desert world that was small, out of the way, and poor. These aspects, along with the fact that Tatooine was controlled by the Hutts, ensured that the Trade Federation had no presence on the world.

Shortly after their landing, Qui-Gon and Obi-Wan

had both acknowledged that they felt a disturbance in the Force. Obi-Wan had remained with the ship while Qui-Gon led a small party to obtain a replacement hyperdrive from a parts dealership in Mos Espa. After that, the detour to Tatooine had taken a series of even stranger turns.

Evidently, there was only one working-condition T-14 hyperdrive available in Mos Espa, but its junkdealer owner — Watto, a Toydarian who was immune to Jedi mind tricks — refused to accept the Republic credits that Qui-Gon offered. But Qui-Gon had also encountered a nine-year-old boy, a slave owned by Watto, who wanted to help the Jedi. Much to Obi-Wan's bafflement, Qui-Gon had endorsed the boy's plan to compete in a Podrace so that he might win a cash prize, which he would then donate for the purchase of the hyperdrive. Apparently, the boy's mother — also Watto's slave — had supported this plan, too.

But that was only part of the story. The night before the Podrace, Qui-Gon had discreetly acquired a blood sample from the boy and transmitted the sample's data to Obi-Wan. Using an analysis device in the starship, Obi-Wan had confirmed that the boy had a midi-chlorian count that was over 20,000 per cell, which was higher than Master Yoda's.

Obi-Wan wondered how such a thing could be possible. *Could the boy be stronger with the Force than Yoda?* Although he understood why Qui-Gon would find the boy intriguing, he also wondered if the boy had become a distraction to their mission.

What could Qui-Gon be thinking? Even with that kind of midi-chlorian count, the boy's too old to begin Jedi training. It's not as if we can do anything beyond possibly liberating him from the Toydarian's ownership.

As things had turned out, the boy won the Podrace and also his freedom. Following the race, Qui-Gon had returned to the starship and delivered the necessary parts, but then declared that he was going back to Mos Espa for "some unfinished business," and instructed Obi-Wan to install the hyperdrive unit.

Which Obi-Wan had done. The ship was ready to launch. They were just waiting for Qui-Gon.

Where is he?

The disturbance in the Force was almost tangible, as if an ominous current charged the air. Obi-Wan rose from his seat on the bridge and glanced at the ship's pilot, Ric Olié, who had so skillfully guided them through the blockade at Naboo. Olié appeared relatively composed as he checked his instrument console, completely oblivious to the disturbance Obi-Wan sensed.

Suddenly the door behind them slid open. Obi-Wan turned to see a young, blond-haired boy in ragged clothes lead the Queen's head of security Captain Panaka and handmaiden Padmé Naberrie onto the bridge.

"Qui-Gon's in trouble!" Panaka said.

Because the Queen's safety was the top priority of the mission, Obi-Wan looked to Ric Olié and said, "Take off." As Olié's fired up the engines, Obi-Wan hunkered down beside the pilot and peered through the viewport. Outside, a short distance from the starship, he saw two figures engaged in a lightsaber duel. One figure was Qui-Gon. The other was a black-robed humanoid wielding a red lightsaber.

"Over there," Obi-Wan instructed the pilot. "Fly low."

The starship lifted off the ground and traveled fast toward Qui-Gon's position. Olié retracted the landing gear but left the portside hatch open and its boarding ramp extended. Obi-Wan kept his eyes on the duel. The sweeping blades had become a furious, deadly blur as they smashed again and again at each other. He could only imagine the identity and origin of Qui-Gon's opponent, or where the creature had learned to fight with a lightsaber, but he had never seen Qui-Gon engaged with such a deadly adversary.

Obi-Wan lost sight of Qui-Gon as the ship traveled over the duelists, but then Olié pointed to a monitor and said, "He's onboard!" The monitor displayed an interior view of the forward hold. Qui-Gon had leapt onto the boarding ramp and rolled into the rapidly rising starship.

Obi-Wan raced for the forward hold, the boy following at his heels. Entering the hold, they found R2-D2 beside Qui-Gon's supine form. The boy cried out, "Are you all right?"

"I think so," Qui-Gon answered breathlessly as he pushed himself up to a seated position. Obi-Wan and the boy crouched down beside him.

"What was it?" Obi-Wan asked.

"I'm not sure," Qui-Gon replied, still gasping, "but it was well-trained in the Jedi arts."

R2-D2 emitted a worried beep, and then Qui-Gon continued, "My guess is it was after the Queen."

The boy's eyes went wide with worry at this, and he exclaimed, "What are we gonna do about it?"

Obi-Wan glanced at the boy. *We?*

Qui-Gon sighed, then faced Anakin and said, "We shall be patient." Then he gestured from the boy to his apprentice and said, "Anakin Skywalker, meet Obi-Wan Kenobi."

"Hi," Anakin said as he pumped Obi-Wan's hand. "Are you a Jedi, too?"

Obi-Wan smiled politely and nodded.

Anakin smiled back. "Pleased to meet you."

He looks so . . . ordinary, Obi-Wan thought. Despite the fact that Jedi were trained from an early age to know that people as well as things were not always what they appeared, Obi-Wan would never have guessed or imagined that the boy beside him might be more powerful than Master Yoda.

After delivering Queen Amidala to Coruscant, Obi-Wan and Qui-Gon brought Anakin to the Jedi Temple. There, the small, green-skinned Jedi Master Yoda, Mace Windu, and their ten fellow members of the Jedi Council were alarmed to hear Qui-Gon's account of his duel on Tatooine. For a thousand years, the Jedi Order had believed that their deadliest enemies, the Sith, were extinct, but after listening to Qui-Gon, they suspected that the Sith had at long last resurfaced.

The Jedi Council and Obi-Wan were even more astonished when Qui-Gon asserted his belief that Anakin Skywalker had been conceived by the midi-chlorians, and that he was the Chosen One, a Jedi who would fulfill an ancient prophecy to destroy the Sith and bring balance to the Force. Despite the fact that most Jedi were brought into the Jedi Order at infancy, the Jedi Council reluctantly agreed to test Anakin's powers.

While the tests were in progress, Obi-Wan and Qui-Gon adjourned to a Temple balcony. The sun was setting over Galactic City, and there was heavy air traffic in the sky. Obi-Wan said, "The boy will not pass the Council's tests, Master. He's too old."

Qui-Gon replied. "Anakin will become a Jedi, I promise you."

"Do not defy the Council, Master . . . not again."

"I shall do what I must, Obi-Wan."

"If you just follow the code, you would *be* on the Council. They will not go along with you this time."

Qui-Gon placed his hand on Obi-Wan's shoulder and said, "You still have much to learn, my young apprentice."

Obi-Wan gazed out across the surrounding sky-scrapers. "What if the boy decides he wants to be with his mother?"

"That would be Anakin's choice," Qui-Gon said. "However, I've already taken a step to help his mother. I've arranged for a courier to go to Tatooine and deliver a Tobal lens to Shmi Skywalker."

"A Tobal lens?" Obi-Wan said. "You mean the crystal used to convert heat to light, the type used to power Renatta photon drives?"

Qui-Gon nodded. "The Toydarian who owns Shmi won't accept Republic credits, and he would be suspicious, to say the least, if Shmi suddenly had any large amount of currency to buy her freedom. However, I believe that if Shmi acquired an item such as a Tobal lens, she would recognize its value as a bargaining chip."

Obi-Wan shook his head. "You can be most baffling, Master."

Qui-Gon shrugged. "As I said, you have much to learn."

*   *   *

41

After the tests were done, Obi-Wan and Qui-Gon rejoined Anakin before the Council. As Obi-Wan had predicted, the Council deemed Anakin too old to become a Jedi. Yoda said the boy would *not* be trained.

"He *is* the Chosen One," Qui-Gon maintained. "You must see it."

Yoda closed his large, wise eyes and tilted his small head back. "Mmm. Clouded, this boy's future is."

Obi-Wan sensed what the members of the Council were thinking. *They all believe Anakin is dangerous.*

"I will train him, then," Qui-Gon said, calmly but still defiantly. Stepping beside Anakin, he placed his hands on the boy's shoulders and proclaimed, "I take him as my Padawan learner."

Indicating Obi-Wan, Yoda said "An apprentice, you *have*, Qui-Gon. Impossible, to take on a second."

"The code forbids it," added Mace Windu.

Qui-Gon said, "Obi-Wan is ready."

Facing Yoda, Obi-Wan stepped forward to stand beside Qui-Gon and declared, "I am ready to face the trials."

"Our *own* counsel we will keep on who is ready," Yoda said.

Qui-Gon said, "He is headstrong, and he has much to learn about the living Force, but he is capable. There is little more he will learn from me."

Obi-Wan glared at Qui-Gon. *First he says I still have much to learn, and now he says this?*

"Decided later young Skywalker's fate will be," Yoda said.

Mace Windu announced that the Senate was voting for a new Supreme Chancellor, and that Queen Amidala planned to return to Naboo and put pressure on the Trade Federation to end the blockade. The Council assigned Qui-Gon and Obi-Wan to escort Amidala home, and allowed Qui-Gon to take Anakin with him.

As Obi-Wan and Qui-Gon prepared to board Amidala's starship with Anakin and R2-D2, Obi-Wan argued with Qui-Gon. "It is not disrespect, Master, it is the truth."

"From your point of view," Qui-Gon countered.

"The boy is *dangerous,*" Obi-Wan said. Referring to the Jedi Council, he added, "They all sense it. Why can't you?"

"His fate is uncertain. He's not dangerous. The Council will decide Anakin's future. That should be enough for you. Now get on board."

Shortly after arriving on Naboo, while Queen Amidala sought military aid from the Naboo's indigenous Gungan warriors, Obi-Wan conferred with Qui-Gon at the edge of a green forest. Obi-Wan said, "I'm . . . I'm sorry for my behavior, Master. It's not my place to disagree with you about the boy. And I *am* grateful you think I'm ready to take the trials."

"You've been a good apprentice, Obi-Wan,"

Qui-Gon said with a smile. "And you're a much wiser man than I am. I foresee you will become a great Jedi Knight."

At Theed, a city on Naboo, Obi-Wan and Qui-Gon became separated from Anakin when they were attacked by the same black-clad warrior they had encountered on Tatooine. The mysterious enemy, whose yellow-eyed face bore jagged red and black tattoos, quickly revealed that his lightsaber had not one blade, but two. He spun and whipped at the Jedi with intense ferocity, and it was all they could do to keep up with him.

The duel lasted several brutal minutes, taking the Jedi and their deadly foe from the Theed hangar to the city's immense power generator. As they moved through a security hallway, the three combatants found themselves temporarily barred from each other by a series of energized barriers. The barriers lifted, allowing Qui-Gon to catch up with their opponent at the edge of the power generator's virtually fathomless core, but before Obi-Wan could reach his Master's side, the energy barrier reactivated to stop him in his tracks.

And then the creature drove his lightsaber straight through Qui-Gon's chest. Obi-Wan shouted as he saw his Master's body crumple at the core's edge. The moment that the energy barrier dropped, Obi-Wan raced forward to attack.

The enemy was incredibly fast. None of Obi-Wan's training had prepared him to deal with an opponent like this. They hammered and spun at each other relentlessly, moving back and forth along the core's edge. Although Obi-Wan wasn't certain that his Master was dead, he tried to steer his opponent away from the area where Qui-Gon lay motionless on the floor, his lightsaber resting a short distance from his fingertips. Obi-Wan slashed through the handle of his opponent's weapon, deactivating one of the blades, but the black-clad figure held tight to his own lightsaber's still-operating half and continued fighting.

Then the foe used the Force to push at Obi-Wan, striking him with such an impact that he released his lightsaber as he tumbled over the edge and into the core. Obi-Wan reached fast to grab a metal protuberance just below the core's upper rim. He was still clinging to the rung when his opponent kicked Obi-Wan's fallen lightsaber into the core. He watched helplessly as his lightsaber fell past him and plunged into the core's depths.

Obi-Wan dangled, his arms straining to maintain a grip. Above him, the demonic figure chopped at the air with his red-bladed lightsaber, taunting and daring Obi-Wan to make one final, desperate move. And then Obi-Wan remembered Qui-Gon's position, and the lightsaber by his side.

Using the Force, Obi-Wan summoned Qui-Gon's lightsaber into the air at the same moment that he kicked at the core's cylindrical wall, launching himself up and out of the core. Obi-Wan caught Qui-Gon's lightsaber and activated it as he sailed over his opponent. The dark figure spun as Obi-Wan landed and swung Qui-Gon's blade, and the creature's evil, tattooed face contorted into an expression of surprise. And then it was the dark figure's turn to tumble into the pit, and as he fell, his neatly cleaved body separated, bounced off the core's walls, and vanished.

Obi-Wan ran to Qui-Gon and carefully elevated his Master's head. Qui-Gon muttered, "No, it — it's too late. . . ."

"No!" Obi-Wan said, his own voice almost a whimper.

"Obi-Wan," Qui-Gon gasped as his eyes locked on his apprentice's face. "Promise — promise me you will train the boy."

"Yes, Master."

Qui-Gon's fingers trembled as he reached up to brush Obi-Wan's cheek, and then he said, "He *is* the Chosen One. He . . . will bring balance. Train him."

Obi-Wan nodded. His Master closed his eyes and died in his arms.

Obi-Wan had long known that all apprentice-ships, one way or another, eventually came to an end.

He knew that Jedi were not immortal, that life was unpredictable, and that death was inevitable. He had even imagined the possibility that he would outlive his older Master. But nothing in his experience or imagination had prepared him for Qui-Gon's last breath, to see the powerful man's life end with such brutal finality.

Obi-Wan lowered his head. He felt stunned and deflated, and uncertain of what to do next. For so many years, he had followed Qui-Gon's lead, but now he was without a Master—and much sooner than he had ever anticipated. He had never felt so alone, as if he had not only lost his closest friend, but his purpose, too. All he could do was try to honor the Jedi who had trained him.

Then he remembered the promise he had made to Qui-Gon.

Obi-Wan realized that his Master had not left him alone, and that he had an entirely new purpose to fulfill.

After becoming separated from the Jedi on Naboo, Anakin Skywalker unintentionally used his temporary hiding space — the cockpit of an N-1 starfighter — to not only engage the Trade Federation invaders but destroy their droid control ship in Naboo's orbit. The loss of the control ship brought a swift end to the battle.

Anakin rejoined Obi-Wan just as a transport from Coruscant arrived at Theed. The former Chancellor Palpatine, who had just been elected Supreme Chancellor, led Yoda and the other members of the Jedi Council in a procession from the landed transport. Stopping before Obi-Wan and Anakin, Palpatine said, "We are indebted to you for your bravery, Obi-Wan Kenobi." Then Palpatine lowered his gaze to Anakin and added, "And you, young Skywalker. We will watch your career with great interest." He clapped the boy on the shoulder, then walked on to confer with Queen Amidala.

Later, as the sun was setting over Theed, Obi-Wan met with Yoda in a chamber at the Queen's palace. The room was lined with tall windows that looked out upon skies displaying a wide range of indigo, castle-like clouds. Obi-Wan knelt on the ornately inlaid floor while Yoda, holding a short walking staff, paced back and forth.

Yoda said, "Confer on you, the level of Jedi Knight, the council does." Stopping to face Obi-Wan, he continued, "But agree with your taking this boy as your Padawan learner . . . *I* do not."

"Qui-Gon believed in him," Obi-Wan said.

Yoda sighed. "The Chosen One, the boy may be. Nevertheless, grave danger I fear in his training."

"Master Yoda, I gave Qui-Gon my word. I *will* train Anakin."

"Ohh!" Yoda grunted, then turned and resumed pacing.

"Without the approval of the Council, if I must."

Facing away from Obi-Wan, Yoda said, "Qui-Gon's defiance I sense in you. Need that you do not." He paused, then added, "Agree with you, the Council does." Turning to face Obi-Wan again, he said, "Your apprentice, Skywalker will be."

A funeral pyre was prepared for Qui-Gon Jinn on Theed. All the members of the Jedi Council were in attendance, as were Palpatine, Queen Amidala, other dignitaries of Naboo, and the droid R2-D2. Obi-Wan stood beside Anakin, who was unaware of his recent conversation with Yoda. Anakin had believed that Qui-Gon might look after him, and Obi-Wan could tell from the boy's pained expression that he believed his own future had died with Qui-Gon.

Lifting his gaze to Obi-Wan, Anakin asked, "What will happen to me now?"

Obi-Wan had not changed his belief that the boy was dangerous, but he also knew that Qui-Gon would not have wasted his last words on anything insignificant. If Qui-Gon had believed that Anakin was the Chosen One, then Obi-Wan felt compelled to at least allow the possibility. He had to trust that Qui-Gon had been right about Anakin, that the boy *could* be trained, because otherwise . . . Obi-Wan suddenly realized he couldn't even consider an alternative. *I won't fail Qui-Gon.*

"The Council have granted me permission to train you," Obi-Wan said solemnly. "You *will* be a Jedi. I promise."

And with that, Anakin's fate was sealed.

CHAPTER THREE

Obi-Wan was surprised and annoyed when he didn't find Anakin in his quarters at the Jedi Temple on Coruscant. *He's supposed to be practicing his meditation exercises,* Obi-Wan thought. *Where could he be?*

Several weeks had passed since Obi-Wan had taken Anakin as his Padawan. Although Anakin was mostly eager to please, his impulsive nature frequently tried Obi-Wan's patience. Anakin had been repeatedly instructed not to leave his quarters without first notifying Obi-Wan of his destination, but three Jedi Masters had already found the boy wandering and exploring various area of the Temple. *There are some rules he simply must obey,* Obi-Wan thought. *Why won't he listen to me?*

Outside Anakin's quarters stretched a long corridor with windows that overlooked the megalopolis of Coruscant City. Obi-Wan had walked only a short distance through the corridor when he spied two figures beyond an open doorway, standing on an outdoor balcony and facing away from him. One figure was Anakin. The other was a lean male humanoid, about Obi-Wan's height, who wore a bizarre, head-concealing goggled mask, and a belted tunic over arm and leg wrappings that left no flesh exposed; attached to his belt were two lightsabers.

As Obi-Wan approached the balcony, he caught Anakin in the middle of asking a stream of questions while the masked figure stood silently, watching the stars emerge over the vast cityscape. "You're from Tatooine, too?" Anakin said to his unresponsive companion. "Can you understand Basic? You might not believe this, but not too long ago, I actually saved a Tusken Raider's life! I found him when I was out in the Xelric Draw. He was a bit bigger than you. Maybe he's a friend of yours? Do you know where the Xelric Draw is? Or maybe your people have another name for it? Did you ever see — ?"

Obi-Wan stepped out onto the balcony and said, "Good evening."

Both Anakin and the masked humanoid turned to face Obi-Wan. Anakin said, "Hello, Obi-Wan — I mean, Master." Then he exclaimed, "Oh! I'm sorry I didn't tell you where I was. I just wanted to, uh, stretch my legs, but then I met, um —" Anakin gestured to the masked figure beside him.

Obi-Wan bowed slightly and said, "I am Obi-Wan Kenobi."

Before the figure could respond, Anakin interjected, "I think he's a Tusken Raider from Tatooine!" Pointing to the weapons at the Tusken's belt, Anakin added, "But he's a Jedi too, like us. Only he has *two* lightsabers."

Indeed, the quiet figure on the balcony was, by all appearances, a Tusken Raider. Obi-Wan could see his own reflection as he peered into the red lenses of the Tusken Jedi's goggles. "Please forgive my impetuous Padawan's manners," Obi-Wan said. "We welcome you to the Jedi Order, A'Sharad Hett."

The masked figure bowed back. Anakin looked at Obi-Wan and said, "You know his name?"

Obi-Wan nodded. He had already been briefed about the recent mission of the Jedi Ki-Adi-Mundi, who had been sent to Tatooine to investigate a report of a Tusken Raider who wielded a lightsaber. The "Tusken" was in fact Sharad Hett, a Jedi of almost legendary status who — along with his illustrious lightsaber — had mysteriously vanished just over fifteen years earlier. According to Ki-Adi-Mundi, it was by the will of the Force that Sharad Hett wound up on Tatooine, adopted the ways of the Tusken Raiders, lived with them, and ultimately became a tribal leader. He also sired a son, A'Sharad Hett, whom he trained in the ways of the Jedi.

Tragically, during Ki-Adi-Mundi's mission, Sharad Hett was mortally wounded by the bounty hunter Aurra Sing. Sharad Hett's last request was for Ki-Adi-Mundi to take fifteen-year-old A'Sharad back to the Jedi Temple to complete his training.

Obi-Wan said, "Your father was a great Jedi, A'Sharad Hett. Your loss is our loss."

A'Sharad Hett bowed his head in return. Through his breath mask, his reply came out as a low rasp. "Thank you, Master Kenobi."

"He talks!" Anakin said. Obi-Wan glared reproachfully at Anakin, who quickly added, "Sorry. It's just that, well, he hadn't said a word up till now."

"I doubt you let him get a word in edgewise," Obi-Wan said. "And speaking of remaining silent, you should be meditating right now, not bothering A'Sharad Hett."

"The boy does not bother me," A'Sharad rasped in a flat, lifeless tone. "He is from Tatooine. To hear him speak of our homeworld . . . his perspective . . . it is interesting."

Obi-Wan smiled at this. "As you were, then," he said. "But just for ten more minutes."

As Obi-Wan left the balcony, he heard Anakin resume speaking. "So, did you ever watch the Podraces? Believe it or not, I won the Boonta Eve Classic! I think some Tuskens shot at me during the race, but I'm guessing that wasn't you, right? Hey, did you ever see a krayt dragon . . . ?"

More than fifteen minutes passed before Anakin finally returned to his quarters, where he found Obi-Wan seated in a chair, waiting for him.

"Sorry I'm late, Master," Anakin said as his door slid shut behind him. "You know A'Sharad Hett's teacher, Ki-Adi-Mundi? Well, he came out to talk with us. They're going on a mission to Malastare! But the reason I'm late is that when Ki-Adi-Mundi found out that I know all about the Podraces on Malastare, he wound up asking me a whole lot of questions about the Phoebos Run. That's the biggest race they have on Malastare, and . . ."

Obi-Wan remained silent but lifted his eyebrows slightly, waiting for Anakin to finish.

"And . . . anyway," Anakin finished, "I just wanted to help."

"I'm sure Ki-Adi-Mundi appreciated that," Obi-Wan said. "I also hope you have found a new friend in A'Sharad Hett. He seems to be a very good listener."

"You can say *that* again."

Obi-Wan was about to reprimand his Padawan for skipping his meditation exercises when he noticed Anakin's expression change, a certain sadness about in his eyes. Anakin said, "I was just thinking about

A'Sharad Hett, wearing that mask and having all his skin covered up . . . never being able to touch things with his fingers or feel air against his face. Why would anyone do that?"

"You know more about Tuskens than I," Obi-Wan said, "but I believe it's simply their tradition."

"But he's a Jedi now."

Obi-Wan shrugged slightly and said, "Then I suppose it's his choice."

"Well, I know *I* could never live like that."

"No one's asking you to," Obi-Wan said with a grin. "However," he continued, more seriously, "I am asking you to keep up with your meditation exercises. They are very important. And so long as it is my duty to train you, so it is your duty to learn from me. Agreed?"

There was a moment of awkward silence, and then Anakin replied, "Yes, Master."

Obi-Wan wasn't sure, but he thought he detected a hint of resentment in Anakin's voice. He hadn't considered that Anakin, because of his experience on Tatooine, might be sensitive to calling anyone *Master*. Obi-Wan sighed, then said, "Please don't think it gives me pleasure to admonish you, Padawan. I can only imagine what it was like for you to grow up as a slave, and I —"

"Do you ever miss your mother?" Anakin interrupted.

The question caught Obi-Wan off guard, but he

recovered fast to answer, "No. No, I don't. I never knew her, not really. I was still an infant when I arrived here, at the Temple."

"Then maybe we can make a deal," Anakin said, and Obi-Wan could tell that the boy was trying to keep his voice from trembling. "You won't feel sorry for me because I was once a slave, and I won't feel sorry for you because you don't miss your mother."

Again, Obi-Wan was not quite sure how to respond, but he decided it was not the time to discuss the dangers of forming personal attachments that might impair a Jedi's judgments and actions. Instead, he rose from his seat and said, "You have reminded me, Padawan, that we have much to learn from each other. For now, please trust that I do not feel sorry for you about your past, or for anything else."

"Then it's a deal," Anakin said, extending his hand to Obi-Wan.

Obi-Wan still questioned the logic of Anakin's deal, but smiled as he shook the boy's hand anyway. "The hour is late," Obi-Wan said. "Perhaps tomorrow you can tell *me* some Podracing stories."

Immediately brightening, Anakin said, "Maybe *we* should go to Malastare too!"

"Patience, Padawan," Obi-Wan said. "Patience."

CHAPTER FOUR

Reflecting on his apprenticeship with Qui-Gon Jinn, Obi-Wan Kenobi knew that he had not always been the most obedient student. In fact, he had even been occasionally foolhardy. Now, ten years after Obi-Wan had begun training Anakin Skywalker, he appreciated Qui-Gon as a teacher even more. As stubborn and independent as Qui-Gon had been regarding the Jedi Code, he also had been patient and generous, two attributes that Obi-Wan found himself increasingly lacking.

Sometimes, it seemed difficult to teach Anakin anything. He had recently turned twenty, and despite Obi-Wan's training, Anakin still let his emotions — especially fear and anger — get the better of him. The faintest praise could make him beam with pride, while the slightest criticism would make him petulant and resentful. Obi-Wan was even more concerned when Anakin confided that he had been having nightmares about his mother dying on Tatooine.

More than once, Obi-Wan mused, *If only Anakin had begun his training as an infant.*

It didn't help that every Jedi at the Temple was aware of Qui-Gon's assertion that Anakin was the Chosen One of prophecy. This made Anakin the focus of more scrutiny than any other Padawan in recent history. Although Anakin never claimed to be the Chosen One, it helped even less that he appeared to enjoy the attention he received because of his association with the prophecy. Ever since the Battle of Naboo, even Supreme Chancellor Palpatine had taken a strong interest in the boy.

Initially, Obi-Wan considered training Anakin as his debt to Qui-Gon. However, over the course of time and numerous missions, Obi-Wan came to regard Anakin as something more than his own personal responsibility. Anakin — impossible as he could be — had become Obi-Wan's friend.

After a mission to Ansion, Obi-Wan and Anakin had just returned to Coruscant when the Jedi Council instructed them to proceed to a high-security Senate apartment building. There, they were scheduled to meet with a Galactic Senator who had recently survived an assassination attempt that had left six others dead. Their assignment was to serve as guards to protect the Senator.

As a lift carried the two Jedi to the skyscraper's

uppermost floors, Obi-Wan noticed that his tall apprentice was nervously fidgeting. Obi-Wan said, "You seem a little on edge."

"Not at all," Anakin said as he smoothed out his long Jedi robes.

Unconvinced, Obi-Wan said, "I haven't felt you this tense since we fell into that nest of gundarks."

Anakin scoffed, "*You* fell into that nightmare, Master, and I rescued you, remember?"

"Oh . . . yes," Obi-Wan replied, and then he chuckled at the memory. Anakin laughed too, but Obi-Wan sensed that his apprentice's anxiety was increasing as they ascended the skyscraper. "You're sweating," Obi-Wan observed. "Relax. Take a deep breath."

"I haven't seen her in ten years, Master."

Obi-Wan grinned and shook his head. The Galactic Senator whom they had been instructed to protect was Padmé Amidala, the former Queen of Naboo. Amidala had been in her teens when she had been elected Queen, and was only a few years older than Anakin. Obi-Wan was aware that Anakin had maintained something of a crush on Amidala for the past decade, and could not help finding some amusement in seeing his apprentice looking so jumpy.

When the lift doors slid open, they were greeted by their old friend Jar Jar Binks, a lanky Gungan they had met just before the Battle of Naboo. Because Obi-Wan now wore a beard and Anakin had grown considerably taller, Jar Jar did not recognize the Jedi at first, but then he locked onto Obi-Wan's eyes and said, "Obi? Obi! Mesa so smilen to seein yousa!"

"Good to see you again, Jar Jar."

Jar Jar turned and called out, "Senator Padmé! Mesa palos here! Lookie, lookie, Senator. Desa Jedi arriven."

Obi-Wan and Anakin followed Jar Jar into a luxurious suite, where they were greeted by Padmé and two of her aides. "It's a great pleasure to see you again, milady," Obi-Wan said as he shook Padmé's hand.

"It has been far too long, Master Kenobi," Padmé replied. And then she lifted her gaze to the tall young man beside Obi-Wan. "Ani?" she said with obvious delight. "My goodness, you've grown."

"So have you," Anakin said sheepishly, then hastily added, "Grown more beautiful, I mean."

Obi-Wan glanced at his awkward apprentice, whose gaze was hopelessly locked onto Padmé's eyes. Anakin continued, "Well, f-for a Senator, I mean."

Padmé laughed. "Ani, you'll always be that little boy I knew on Tatooine."

As the group proceeded to discuss the recent attempt on Padmé's life, Anakin was hardly cooperative. Although he and Obi-Wan had been instructed merely to protect Padmé, he openly promised to find the assassins who had tried to kill her. When Anakin questioned the logic of the Jedi Council's directives to watch over Padmé, Obi-Wan was compelled to reprimand his apprentice before the group, which prompted Anakin to glower.

He's not thinking like a Jedi, Obi-Wan thought ruefully. *He's letting his emotions interfere with our assignment.*

Obi-Wan wondered if the Jedi Council had made a mistake when they had assigned him and Anakin to protect Padmé, but then it hadn't been entirely the Council's decision. It had been Supreme Chancellor Palpatine's idea.

In recent months, numerous former-member worlds of the Republic had allied with the Separatist movement. The Separatists were led by a former Jedi, the charismatic Count Dooku. Dooku expounded that the Galactic Senate was corrupt beyond repair, and promised a new unified government throughout the galaxy. Because many Senators from the remaining Republic worlds believed they would soon be vulnerable to the Separatists, they endorsed the creation of an army to defend the Republic. The reason that Padmé Amidala had traveled to Coruscant was to cast her vote against the Military Creation Act because she knew that the formation of an army would almost certainly lead to civil war.

R2-D2 had remained with Padmé since the Battle of Naboo, and the astromech droid had accompanied her to Coruscant. As events turned out, R2-D2's presence in Padmé's suite was most fortunate, for while Obi-Wan and Anakin argued about their orders and the best way to protect Padmé, it was the R2-D2 who alerted them that the suite had been infiltrated.

A mysterious assassin had released a pair of small, deadly arthropods into Padmé's bedroom. Using his lightsaber, Anakin swiftly killed the creatures, and then both he and Obi-Wan raced out into the night to pursue the assassin.

The Jedi became separated and Anakin dropped his lightsaber during the dizzying, perilous chase that carried them across and through multiple levels of Galactic City. Obi-Wan was able to recover his apprentice's weapon, and caught up with Anakin outside a gambling club called the Outlander. Pointing into the Outlander's wide, brightly illuminated doorway, Anakin said, "She went into the club, Master."

"Patience," Obi-Wan said. "Use the Force. Think."

"Sorry, Master."

"He went in there to hide, not to run."

"Yes, Master."

Obi-Wan held up Anakin's lightsaber and said, "Next time, try not to lose it."

"Yes, Master."

"This weapon is your life."

Anakin took the weapon and said, "I try, Master."

As Anakin followed him into the Outlander, Obi-Wan muttered, "Why do I get the feeling you're going to be the death of me?"

"Don't say that, Master. You're the closest thing I have to a father."

Anakin's words did not make Obi-Wan sympathetic. Without breaking his stride into the crowded club, he said, "Then why don't you listen to me?"

"I am trying."

They stopped to survey the crowd. The patrons were talking and drinking, gambling and playing hologames. Obi-Wan asked, "Can you see him?"

"I think *he* is a *she*, and I think she is a changeling."

"In that case, be extra careful." Then Obi-Wan tilted his head to Anakin and added, "Go and find her."

"Where are *you* going, Master?"

"For a drink," Obi-Wan replied. Leaving Anakin, he stepped over to the bar and signaled the bartender. A moment later, the bartender placed a small glass filled with luminescent blue liquid in front of Obi-Wan, who said, "Thank you."

A young humanoid, a Balosar with flexible antene-palps that extended from his stylishly filthy hair, edged up beside Obi-Wan and rapidly stammered, "You wanna buy some death sticks?"

To any respectable person, the Balosar would have been an annoyance. To Obi-Wan, he was only a slight distraction, but hardly a welcome one. Obi-Wan did not want to endanger the Balosar by allowing him to remain by his side, nor encourage him to peddle his wares elsewhere. Obi-Wan kept his eyes forward, but made a slight gesture with his right hand as he replied, "You don't want to sell me death sticks."

The Balosar was unaware that Obi-Wan was manipulating his mind. He looked slightly confused, then thoughtful as he answered, "I don't want to sell you death sticks."

"You want to go home and rethink your life."

"I want to go home and rethink my life." The Balosar stepped away from the bar, leaving his unfinished drink behind. As he walked away, Obi-Wan's eyes flicked over the patrons in front of him, and left his back exposed. He did this deliberately. *Let her think I can't see her coming.*

Despite the noise, the crowd, the lights, the strange mix of smells in the air, and every other distraction, Obi-Wan sensed the danger that approached him from behind. He drew his lightsaber and activated its blade as he spun, neatly cleaving through the assassin's right arm before she even had the chance to fire her blaster. Her forearm, still holding the blaster, sailed to the floor as she cried out and fell back against the game table.

Anakin moved fast to Obi-Wan's side and leveled his gaze at the astonished patrons. "Easy," he said. "Jedi business. Go back to your drinks."

The assassin wore a visored helmet and a dark violet form-fitting bodysuit with a flexible armorweave jerkin. She appeared to be a human female. Anakin opened a back door that led to an alley and Obi-Wan hauled her through the doorway and outside. Anakin glanced up and down the alley as Obi-Wan eased the woman's body onto the hard ground. Obi-Wan asked, "Do you know who it was you were trying to kill?"

The woman groaned, then said, "It was a Senator from Naboo."

"And who hired you?"

"It was just a job."

Anakin leaned down and said in a gentle, soothing tone, "Who hired you? Tell us." But when the woman did not immediately reply, Anakin's face contorted with anger and he snarled, "Tell us now!"

She said, "It was a bounty hunter called —"

Before she could finish, a small, dart-like projectile buried itself suddenly into her neck. Obi-Wan and Anakin turned their heads to gaze up in the direction of the projectile's trajectory. They saw an armored figure, a man wearing a jetpack, launching up and away from a distant rooftop before he vanished into the night sky of the city.

The bounty hunter?

Obi-Wan returned his gaze to the woman he held, and saw that Anakin was right: she wasn't human. She was a changeling, a shape-shifting Clawdite. Her face reverted to its relaxed state, revealing somewhat lumpy, heavily scarred features. She gasped, "Wee shahnit . . . sleemo." Her wide, heavy-lidded eyes fell closed and she died in Obi-Wan's arms.

Obi-Wan pulled the projectile from her neck and held it out so Anakin could examine it, too. It was a nasty piece of work, an injector-needle tip with stabilizing fins for long-range shots and embedding prongs to anchor into the target. "Toxic dart," Obi-Wan said. He looked back toward the distant rooftop that had served as a launch pad for the Clawdite's killer, and he thought, *He could have shot us, too — if he'd wanted.*

Obi-Wan turned to Anakin and said, "Her last words. Did you understand them?"

"She spoke in Huttese," Anakin said. "She said, 'Bounty hunter slimeball.'"

Obi-Wan had no idea of the armored bounty hunter's identity, but he did not question the fact that the man was very, very dangerous.

Obi-Wan was not surprised when the Jedi Council instructed him to track down the bounty hunter and identify his employers. However, their decision to have Anakin escort Senator Amidala back to her homeworld, for her own safety, did cause him some concern. It would be Anakin's first assignment without his Master, and despite all of his abilities, he was also arrogant, and Obi-Wan didn't think he was ready. But the Council was confident in their decision, and Obi-Wan personally escorted Anakin, Padmé, and R2-D2 to the Coruscant spaceport and waiting freighter that would take them to Naboo.

Obi-Wan began his investigation by trying to identify the toxic dart that he had removed from the Clawdite's neck. After the analysis droids in the Jedi Archives failed to provide any useful information about the dart, he realized he would have to consult a different sort of expert.

Obi-Wan had kept in touch with Dexter Jettster over the years, and he was fortunate in that he did not have to go far to find the well-traveled Besalisk. Dexter was currently the proprietor and head cook at Dex's Diner in CoCo Town, a commercial district in the upper levels of Galactic City on Coruscant. Dexter greeted his old friend with a big hug. After they settled down in a diner booth that looked out on a busy street, Obi-Wan placed the dart on the table in front of Dexter.

"Well, whattaya know!" Dexter exclaimed as he picked up the dart. "I ain't seen one of these since I was prospectin' on Subterrel, beyond the Outer Rim."

"Can you tell me where it came from?"

"This baby belongs to them cloners. What you got here is a Kamino saberdart."

Obi-Wan had always been amazed by Dexter's powers of observation as well as his keen memory. He said,

"I wonder why it didn't show up in the analysis archives."

Brushing his thick fingers along the dart's stabilizing fins, Dexter said, "It's these funny little cuts on the side that give it away. Those analysis droids only focus on symbols. Huh! I should think that you Jedi would have more respect for the difference between knowledge and . . ." Dexter chuckled before he finished, ". . . wisdom."

Obi-Wan grinned and replied, "Well, if droids could think, there'd be none of us here, would there?" Taking the dart back from Dexter, he continued, "Kamino. I'm not familiar with it. Is it in the Republic?"

"No, no. It's beyond the Outer Rim. I'd say about, uh, twelve parsecs, outside the Rishi Maze. Should be easy to find. Even for those droids in your archives."

But Dexter was wrong about Kamino being easy to find. After Obi-Wan left Dex's Diner, he returned to the Jedi Archives and quickly ascertained that there were no records for Kamino at all. However, when he examined holographic star charts to find the location that Dexter had described, he did detect an apparently invisible source of gravity where a solar system *should* have been.

But solar systems don't just disappear. What happened to it?

Obi-Wan decided to consult Yoda. He found Yoda teaching a class of young Jedi initiates. They were learning how to use the Force, testing their developing skills with lightsabers against hovering remotes. After Obi-Wan explained his dilemma about the missing solar system and planet to Yoda, Yoda encouraged him to display the holographic star chart on a map reader for the entire class to see.

Obi-Wan placed a small, silver ball on the map reader, and a three-dimensional view of hundreds of stars filled the central area of the room. He pointed out the approximate location of the missing solar system. Yoda said, "Hmm. Gravity's silhouette remains, but the star and all the planets . . . disappeared they have." Facing his students, he asked, "How can this be? Hmm?"

It was one of Yoda's pupils, a little boy, who answered. "Master? Because someone erased it from the archive memory."

Obi-Wan smiled. The boy had arrived at the most logical solution, but it was one that Obi-Wan hadn't even entertained. *Only a Jedi could have erased the memory. Who would have done such a thing? And why?*

Obi-Wan used a Delta-7 starfighter to travel to the "missing" solar system, where he found the water-world of Kamino. He landed his starfighter on a rain-spattered platform close to the administrative center of Tipoca City, a cluster of enormous domed structures that were elevated by massive stilts above the constantly stormy sea.

The Kaminoans were long-necked amphibians. Obi-Wan was surprised when he was told that Kamino's prime minister, Lama Su, had been expecting a Jedi to arrive. He was led to Lama Su, who revealed that ten years earlier, the Jedi Master Sifo-Dyas had commissioned the Kaminoans to produce, train, and outfit a clone army for the Republic. According to Lama Su, the Kaminoans had been waiting for the Jedi to take delivery of Sifo-Dyas's order ever since.

Obi-Wan found this information baffling. He recalled that Sifo-Dyas had been killed almost a decade ago, and could not imagine why Sifo-Dyas or any other Jedi would have made such an arrangement with the Kaminoans. *Even if Sifo-Dyas had anticipated the threat of the Separatist movement, he certainly didn't have the resources to finance a clone army!* But Obi-Wan also sensed it was best to play along for the time being, and pretended that he had indeed arrived on Kamino to inspect the clones.

As Lama Su guided Obi-Wan on a tour of the vast, multi-level cloning facility, Obi-Wan saw thousands of clones. All of them appeared to be identical dark-haired human males, at various stages of growth up through age twenty. Lama Su explained that growth acceleration allowed the clones to mature faster while genetic modifications made them less independent than the original host, the man who had served as the clones' template.

"And who was the original host?" Obi-Wan asked.

"A bounty hunter called Jango Fett," Lama Su replied.

Believing that he was closing in on the man who'd fired the saberdart on Coruscant, Obi-Wan asked casually, "And where is this bounty hunter now?"

"Oh, we keep him here."

Obi-Wan readily accepted the offer to meet Jango Fett. Although he knew it was highly probable that Fett was the same bounty hunter behind the attempted assassinations on Coruscant, he did not believe he would require any reinforcements.

A few standard days after his first encounter with Jango Fett, and many light-years away from Kamino, Obi-Wan found himself suspended in the air, trapped within a force field chamber of a droid factory on the planet Geonosis. He thought, *Now would be a good time for some reinforcements to arrive!*

On Kamino, Obi-Wan had met Jango Fett as well as the man's "son," an unmodified ten-year-old clone named Boba. Obi-Wan had quickly determined that Fett was indeed the armored bounty hunter he'd seen on Coruscant, but had been unable to stop the Fetts from escaping Kamino. Fortunately, he had secured a tracer beacon onto Fett's starship, a Kuat Systems *Firespray*-class interceptor, which enabled him to follow the ship to Geonosis.

A red, rocky planet ringed by asteroids, Geonosis was inhabited by the semi-insectoid Geonosians. Obi-Wan had stealthily infiltrated a towering Geonosian hive to discover the Separatist leader Count Dooku engaged in a secret meeting with officials from various worlds. He learned that the Neimoidian Trade Federation was behind the assassination attempts on Padmé Amidala, and that the Commerce Guilds and the Corporate Alliance had pledged their armies to Dooku. He had also learned that the Trade Federation would soon take delivery of a massive droid army from a Geonosian factory. He had even managed to send a transmission with most of this information to Anakin, who — for reasons unknown to Obi-Wan — had left Naboo and gone to Tatooine.

But then Obi-Wan had been attacked by droids and was captured.

Now, suspended in a force field with energy binders wrapped around his wrists and ankles, Obi-Wan wondered if Anakin had managed to relay his transmission to the Jedi Council. As he hung in the air of the hive chamber, all he could do was wait.

Little did he know that within a few short hours, the Jedi would arrive with clone troops from Kamino, and the Clone Wars would begin.

Ben Kenobi had told Luke Skywalker that he had served with Luke's father, Anakin, during the Clone Wars, so when Luke finally found an entry about the Clone Wars in Ben's journal, he became so excited he almost forgot about the furnace he had set up inside Ben's hut. He was using the furnace to create the gem for his new lightsaber, and really couldn't hurry the process, so he had been reading Ben's journal while waiting for the furnace to reach its full temperature.

Luke's knowledge of the Clone Wars was relatively limited. Most of the "facts" came from old datatapes, but only those that had been authorized by the Empire. Still, he knew that the Jedi Knights had led clone armies on behalf of the Galactic Republic against the Confederacy of Independent Systems. In the end, the Confederacy lost, the Jedi were accused of attempting to take over the Republic, and the Republic's leader, Palpatine, was proclaimed Emperor. According to Ben, *it was Darth Vader who helped the Empire hunt down and destroy the Jedi.*

After checking the furnace, Luke returned his attention to the journal and the entry he had found, and started reading it from the beginning. Ben had made a notation that indicated the entry was almost twenty years old.

Officially, the Clone Wars began at the Battle of Geonosis, for it was there that the Jedi Knights first utilized the clone troops that had been commissioned to fight on behalf of the Republic against the Separatists' droid militia. Although the Separatists were defeated at Geonosis, they quickly regrouped as the Confederacy of Independent Systems. The galaxy plunged into a civil war that would last over three terrible years.

My fellow Jedi and I were conscripted as generals for the Grand Army of the Republic. Like the worlds of the Republic, the Jedi were also soon divided, as some refused to fight and abandoned the Jedi Order.

Unofficially, the Clone Wars began at least ten years before the Battle of Geonosis, when — I eventually realized — the Sith Lords began taking measures to ensure that the Republic would one day have reason to require an army.

The Sith Lords engineered every aspect of the Clone Wars, controlling both the Republic and the Confederacy and pitting them against each other, all in an effort to annihilate the Republic and the Jedi Order and claim galactic conquest.

If my words sound like the ravings of a paranoid, crazy hermit, consider the fact that the Sith Lord Darth Vader serves the Emperor, and the Jedi are all but gone.

Luke was disappointed that the entry ended there. While he set the book aside and checked on the furnace again, he wondered why Ben hadn't written more about the Clone Wars. It never occurred to him that Ben might have sometimes wished he couldn't remember the Clone Wars at all.

CHAPTER FIVE

Clone Commander Cody shouted, "Incoming!"

Jedi General Obi-Wan Kenobi already heard the deadly crescendo of approaching missiles. His division of the Republic Grand Army, the 7th Sky Corps, had just gained ground at a public park in a city square. They were on Farquar III, a planet that had recently allied with the Confederacy of Independent Systems.

Cody's helmeted head turned to see Obi-Wan's hand signal: right hand extended, two fingers aimed at the sky, followed by a swift chop in the direction from which the missiles were fired.

Cody swung his gaze up at the armored clone troopers who were positioned on the wide roof of the building behind him and Kenobi. Holding his blaster rifle in his right hand, Cody signaled with his left to the anti-missile unit to train their laser cannons at the incoming missiles, and then directed a second unit to target and fire at their attackers.

The first unit calculated the speed and approach of the missiles as they raised their cannons. The second unit did the same as they bounced a signal off two airborne Republic dropships to pinpoint their enemy's position.

The incoming missiles — seven total — entered visual range. Both of Kenobi's anti-missile units fired at their respective targets. A moment later there were five simultaneous explosions overhead. The first unit had missed two missiles.

Obi-Wan dived for cover behind a statue of a poet he had never heard of and threw his gloved hands over his ears. One of the enemy missiles took out Obi-Wan's second anti-missile unit, while the other missile struck an adjacent apartment building. Fragments of missiles, ferrocrete, and clone armor sprayed past Obi-Wan's position.

Uncovering his ears and springing to his feet, Obi-Wan heard a ripple of distant explosions, and hoped his now-decimated second unit had hit their enemy target. Turning to Cody, he shouted, "Status!"

"Scored and burned!" Cody shouted back, but before Obi-Wan could issue his next command, a squad of battle droids marched out of an alley and lurched toward the park. Obi-Wan activated his lightsaber. The droids opened fire, launching a hail of crimson energy bolts into the city square where the 7th Sky Corps had landed less than three minutes earlier.

The Republic's objective was to destroy a Trade Federation-financed droid factory. Unfortunately, the Confederacy had somehow anticipated the Republic Army's arrival. Even worse, during their descent to Farquar III, Obi-Wan had become separated from Anakin as well as Jedi General T'Teknulp, who led their reinforcements.

Obi-Wan leapt away from the statue, rolled across a plot of rubble, and came up standing to swing his light-saber at the fired energy bolts. His blade became nothing more than a blur as he batted away, smacking the bolts back at the approaching droids, cutting them down with their own barrage. But another squad of droids was close behind, marching forward from the same alley.

Obi-Wan thought, not for the first time, *Where are Anakin and T'Teknulp?!*

"Sir!" Cody cried out from behind, jolting Obi-Wan's attention back to the latest round of battle droids, just as they opened fire. Again, Obi-Wan's blade swept and smacked at the energy bolts, sending them back at the droids. He was still swinging at the bolts when six large wheel-like droids rolled out from the alley and spun toward Obi-Wan's position.

Droidekas!

Bouncing over rubble and the remains of the fallen battle droids, the droidekas whipped around to arrange themselves in a circular formation on the ground, then rapidly transformed, activating their spherical deflector shields as they unfolded their double-barreled blaster-cannon arms and dug their tripod foot claws into the street.

The droidekas opened fire into the square. Knowing that neither his lightsaber nor blaster bolts would penetrate the droids' shields, Obi-Wan swung at the incoming bolts, batting them so that they exploded into the ground at the droids' perimeter. The clone troops followed their general's lead, training their DC-15 blaster rifles at the areas of ground around and between the droidekas. The clone troops maintained fire, hammering at the ground as crimson laser bolts whizzed past them and glanced off their armor, while on the roof behind them, the surviving anti-missile unit reloaded their cannons and waited for their general's order.

Obi-Wan hoped to blast the ground out from under the droids and send them crashing below street level. Over the roar of blasters, he angled his arm to the anti-missile team and shouted "Fire!"

Responding with hair-trigger efficiency, the anti-missile team fired their cannons. Four missiles streaked down between the droidekas. The missiles detonated on impact, but instead of tearing a wide hole in the ground, the explosion merely sent ferrocrete flying and knocked the shielded droids away from each other. Launched off their feet but safely contained within their spherical shields, the droids rebounded off the walls of the surrounding buildings like toy bouncing balls, only to roll back to the scorched, battered surface of the street and reassume their deadly circle. The droidekas began firing again.

That didn't go well!

Two clone troopers were hit and went down on either side of Obi-Wan. Wondering what had become of Anakin and their reinforcements, Obi-Wan snapped the comlink from his belt as he ducked behind a wide pylon at the park's entrance gate. He used the established code names for the mission as he said into the comlink, "Kay Six to Tee Eight! Kay Six to Tee Eight!"

"Tee Eight here!" a strangely jovial and high, squeaking voice answered from the comlink. It was General T'Teknulp, a Chadra-Fan Jedi, who always sounded happy no matter what the circumstances. T'Teknulp continued, "Wild greeting! See you in minus five! Tee Eight out!"

Obi-Wan flicked off his comlink. *Wild greeting* meant T'Teknulp's division had encountered enemy forces in planetary orbit, but Obi-Wan couldn't worry too much about that. T'Teknulp had dealt with more than a few *wild greetings* in recent weeks, and had not once been injured. If T'Teknulp said he would be at Obi-Wan's position in less than five minutes, as he had indicated via the comlink, then Obi-Wan trusted T'Teknulp would arrive within five minutes. What worried Obi-Wan was that he doubted his own division could survive for even *one* more minute.

And then he glanced up and saw Anakin.

Anakin was standing in the open hatch of a Republic gunship that was coming in low and fast from the south. Smoke billowed out from the gunship's left stabilizer. *His ship has been hit!* Another enemy missile suddenly appeared in the sky, traveling fast from the city's business district. Obi-Wan's eyes went wide as the missile struck the side of Anakin's gunship.

"Anakin!"

The gunship erupted but Anakin had already leapt away from it. As the shattered gunship spiraled downward, Obi-Wan kept his eyes on his apprentice, watching Anakin's form as he rotated in midair, activated his own lightsaber, and landed on his feet on the roof of a building that adjoined a theater. The ruptured gunship fell sideways and crashed onto a water fountain, killing the vehicle's clone pilot instantly. A split-second after the crash, the gunship exploded, and the power of the blast nearly knocked Obi-Wan off his feet.

The droidekas hit two more clone troopers. Obi-Wan was planning his next move when he saw Anakin run and leap from his landing point to the rooftop of the neighboring theater.

An immense, eight-meter-wide octagonal marquee was affixed to the theater's outer wall above the main entrance, which overlooked the droidekas. As Anakin jumped over the edge of the roof with his lightsaber extended, Obi-Wan — once again batting at the droidekas' fired bolts — realized that Anakin was going for the marquee's structural supports.

Three more clone troopers went down.

Obi-Wan moved quickly. Darting away from his position, he ran fast, weaving back and forth across the park, drawing the droidekas' fire. Lightsaber extended, he continued batting at the energy bolts as he ran, but now, his only intention was to keep the droids occupied and distract them from Anakin's action outside the theater.

Anakin had landed on a window ledge. He gripped his lightsaber in his right hand, and Obi-Wan was glad for the fact that his apprentice had adjusted so well to the prosthetic that had replaced the right arm he'd lost to Count Dooku on Geonosis. Balancing on the ledge, Anakin brought his blade through two of the marquee's thick plastoid anchors. There was an ugly cracking sound as the enormous marquee tilted away from the building. Anakin leapt fast for another ledge and repeated the action with his lightsaber on more anchors. The marquee began to fall to the street below.

The droidekas were still firing at Obi-Wan when the marquee came crashing down on top of them. Although the droids' deflector shields were invulnerable to energy weapons, they could not repel the crushing force of the heavy marquee. The six droids were smashed flat.

At the moment of impact, the clone troops stopped firing. Except for the whooshing sound of the fires that burned amidst the wreckage in the city square, the area was silent.

Anakin scrambled down the side of the theater and landed on top of the fallen marquee just as Obi-Wan arrived beside him. Both had deactivated their lightsabers. Catching his breath, Obi-Wan said, "Well done, Padawan."

Anakin gestured to the marquee beneath them and said, "I'd say it was a smashing performance."

Despite all the destruction and carnage, Obi-Wan couldn't help grinning. But he wagged a finger in mock reproach and said, "Points off for puns."

Anakin scanned the area and said, "Where's T'Teknulp? He was right behind my gunship."

"He had a 'wild greeting,' but he's on his way." Seeing Commander Cody approach, Obi-Wan said, "Cody, inform General T'Teknulp he needn't hurry on our account."

Cody removed his helmet. By now, Obi-Wan was so familiar with Cody that he no longer thought anything of the fact that the clone's features were identical to Jango Fett's. Cody replied, "Sorry, sir. Just received word from the fleet. General T'Teknulp and his division didn't make it."

Obi-Wan was stunned. He lowered his gaze to the ground, then looked up to face Anakin, who was equally staggered by Cody's report. Anakin shook his head and said, "He . . . T'Teknulp . . . he was right behind me."

Cody's eyes flicked from Anakin back to Obi-Wan, then he said, "Orders, sir?"

Obi-Wan thought of all the Jedi who had already died since the Battle of Geonosis. He hoped it wouldn't be long before he and Anakin tracked down Count Dooku and General Grievous, who always seemed three steps ahead of the Jedi.

"Let's get moving," Obi-Wan answered grimly. "We have a droid factory to blow up."

During the Clone Wars, Obi-Wan noticed that Anakin was becoming more focused as a Jedi. One reason for Anakin's change in behavior was that he no longer suffered from nightmares about his mother dying. However, the reason for this was most tragic.

Just before the Battle of Geonosis, Anakin's recurring nightmares had prompted him to disobey orders and travel with Padmé Amidala from Naboo to Tatooine. On the sand planet, Anakin learned that his mother had been freed from her Toydarian owner several years earlier, and that she had married a moisture farmer named Cliegg Lars. The farmer and his family informed Anakin that Shmi had been abducted by the violent, nomadic Tusken Raiders.

Anakin had been unable to save his mother, but

recovered her dead body from the Tusken Raiders' camp and buried her at the Lars homestead. When he left Tatooine, he took C-3PO, a protocol droid that he had constructed in childhood.

Although Obi-Wan had never really known his own family, he did have sympathy for Anakin's loss. And as Anakin's powers grew stronger, Obi-Wan began to believe that his Padawan may have been transformed by the tragedy for the better.

INTERLUDE

Reading Ben Kenobi's journal, Luke Skywalker found another entry that mentioned the Clone Wars. It also mentioned Anakin Skywalker and Darth Vader. Ben had written the entry after the shorter one about the Clone Wars.

Two days ago, on one of my walks, I came across the twisted, withered husk of a short desert plant that had grown in the shadows of a dusty rock formation. Yesterday, I passed the same plant again and noticed it had flowered small white petals, flecked with dark grey. This morning, I was surprised to find the entire plant had vanished. Even though I knew some creature had probably eaten it, I felt a sense of loss that surprised me. And I thought of Asajj Ventress.

I've already written instructions for how to build a lightsaber. Now, I find myself compelled to write something of the enemies who use them.

From what I remember from the history databooks, the Sith have wielded lightsabers for at least four thousand years. They were long believed to have been extinct until just sixteen years ago, when my Master and I dueled with an Iridonian Zabrak who used a double-bladed lightsaber. This Sith killed my Master, and then I killed him in self-defense.

Ten years later, my apprentice Anakin Skywalker and I dueled Count Dooku at the Battle of Geonosis. The leader of the Separatist movement, Dooku was a former Jedi Master who — we realized too late — had turned to the dark side. This was most unfortunate, not only because Dooku had been a revered Jedi, but also because he was a master swordsman. Dooku escaped at the Battle of Geonosis, but not before he informed me that a Sith Lord was manipulating the Galactic Senate. Three devastating years later — after Anakin defeated Dooku in orbit above Coruscant — I would learn that he was telling the truth. The Sith Lord was Supreme Chancellor Palpatine.

Soon after the Battle of Geonosis, Anakin and I had our first encounter with Asajj Ventress. She was a humanoid, hairless with pale skin, who wielded two lightsabers simultaneously. These lightsabers could also be joined at the handles to create a double-bladed weapon. Before she attacked, she told me that she had emerged from misery and suffering, only to find the Jedi she had once worshipped were nothing but "weak, misguided fools." She added that she agreed with Count Dooku, that the galaxy was in need of a Jedi purge.

Asajj Ventress escaped that day, but not before she killed one Jedi and maimed his apprentice. It was obvious by her technique that she had received training from Dooku. Over the course of the Clone Wars, Anakin and I had faced off against Ventress on other worlds. But despite all her fury and murderous inclinations, I always sensed something within her that distinguished her from the Sith Lords: an underlying fear. Mostly, it was a fear of being alone. And I sensed that there was some good in her, some part that had not been corrupted by Dooku. Where the Sith Lords were unquestionably evil, Ventress was simply a slave to the dark side.

She wasn't the only one. General Grievous — another of Dooku's disciples in lightsaber combat — was in command of the Confederacy's droid armies. Grievous was a cyborg who had killed a number of Jedi and taken their lightsabers as trophies. He was capable of wielding four lightsabers simultaneously. All in all, a most unpleasant fellow. I defeated him on Utapau.

And then the Purge began. I would soon learn that I was among the few Jedi to survive, and that Palpatine had taken a new apprentice: my former student, Darth Vader. And because of Darth Vader, Anakin was gone as well.

Eventually, I learned some details of Ventress's history. She was born on Rattaka, an Outer Rim world, so remote that it was unknown to the Republic. She was still a child when her parents were killed by one of the many local warlords. After a Jedi named Ky Narec became stranded on Rattaka, he found the orphaned Ventress and realized she was Force-sensitive. Narec trained Ventress as his apprentice, and apparently trained her relatively well, for together they defeated many criminals. Tragically, a group of warlords killed Narec, and rather than honoring the ways of the Jedi, Ventress sought vengeance. And once again, she was alone. Is it any wonder that she developed such a supreme hatred for the Jedi Order that "abandoned" her Master?

In hindsight, Vader and Ventress had some similar characteristics. Both knew of the loss of loved ones, and had reason to distrust the Republic and the Jedi Order. But when I finally caught up with Vader, I sensed nothing but pure evil about him. For unlike Ventress, Vader was not a victim of unfortunate circumstances. Yes, he had his struggles and his shortcomings, but he was not a weak being who feared abandonment. He was a powerful man who had been given opportunities to better himself, yet he only craved more power, and chose his own path to betray the Jedi and become a Sith. He was my greatest failure.

My duel with Vader was awful in its savagery. In the end, he was more determined to kill me than defend himself, and was blind with fury when I felled him. I left him maimed and burning on the shores of a lava river. To have dealt him a killing blow might have been the merciful thing to do, but I had no mercy for Vader.

Because I am a Jedi, not a coldblooded murderer, all I could do was leave Vader to his fate. Had I killed then and there, I believe I would have taken a step onto the same dark path that he had found so impossible to resist. But by leaving him for dead, I fear I failed yet again, for I soon learned that Vader had survived, in a fashion. Like the late General Grievous, he is mostly machine now, a malevolent construct of pistons and gears, plastoid and wires, his mortal remains fueled by the dark side. The galaxy will never know peace until Darth Vader and the Emperor breathe their last.

It is hard for me to see what the future holds. Fortunately, I have my mission and my ongoing studies of the Force to help me be mindful of the present, as well as the daily rigors of survival on Tatooine. Whatever tomorrow may bring, I must be ready for it.

By the time Luke reached the end of the entry, he realized he'd been holding his breath for over a minute. Exhaling slowly, he returned to the beginning, scanning the text to see if he had missed something. He had never heard of Asajj Ventress, Count Dooku, an Iridonian Zabrak, or any of the battles that Ben had mentioned. But these revelations barely even registered — Luke was frustrated that Ben hadn't written more about Anakin and Vader.

He reread aloud the two lines that had especially commanded his attention: "'. . . Palpatine had taken a new apprentice: my former student, Darth Vader. And because of Darth Vader, Anakin was gone as well.'"

The words sounded hollow in his mouth. Although Ben had not written in so many words that Darth Vader had killed Anakin, that was what Ben had told *him had happened. He wondered just how carefully Ben had chosen his words when he had written that* Anakin was gone.

And then he read again about how Ben — or rather Obi-Wan — had left Vader to die.

Luke had no illusions that Darth Vader was a killer. Vader had also tortured both Princess Leia and Han Solo on different occasions. On Cloud City, Vader had maimed Luke before inviting him to join the dark side and help him overthrow the Emperor. But despite all the horrible things Vader had done, and despite the fact that Ben had no mercy for Vader, Luke was surprised that he felt something other than horror or anger at the thought of the armored Dark Lord of the Sith.

I feel sorry for him.

As the phantom pain chewed at his right wrist, Luke wondered what exactly had happened all those years ago on an unidentified world, along the shores of a lava river.

CHAPTER SIX

"It's over, Anakin!" Obi-Wan shouted from the upper slope of the lava river's shore on the volcanic planet Mustafar. "I have the high ground!"

Anakin was indeed below Obi-Wan's position, standing atop what was left of a floating mining platform that glided over the lava. Glaring at Obi-Wan, Anakin growled, "You underestimate my power."

Obi-Wan had escaped Utapau when his own clone troops — obeying Palpatine's secret Order 66 — had opened fire on him. Leaving Utapau in General Grievous' starfighter, he had followed a coded signal to find temporary refuge on the *Tantive IV*, the consular starship owned by Bail Organa, a Senator from Alderaan, who was an ally to the Jedi. The *Tantive IV* had also harbored Yoda, who had escaped a similar assassination by clones on the Wookiee homeworld, Kashyyk. Organa delivered Obi-Wan and Yoda back to Coruscant, where they found

the Jedi Temple in ruins, and all the resident Jedi —
even the youngest initiates — lying dead.

And then they had viewed a recording that revealed
Anakin was responsible for the slaughter. They also
discovered Senator Palpatine was a Sith Lord, and that
he had enlisted Anakin to the dark side, and dubbed his
new apprentice as "Darth Vader."

Obi-Wan had gone to Padmé to warn her about
Anakin, and then stowed away in her starship when
she went in search of Anakin. They had landed on
Mustafar, where Anakin had just butchered the leaders
of the Confederacy. When Anakin saw Obi-Wan, he
had become enraged with Padmé and accused them
both of conspiring to kill him. He had tried to strangle
Padmé, and then his fight with Obi-Wan had begun.

The long, grueling duel had carried them far from
the landing pad where Padmé's ship had landed.
Now, the battle had neared its end.

Obi-Wan realized what Anakin was about to do, and
despite all that had recently transpired, he pleaded,
"Don't try it."

Gripping his lightsaber, Anakin leaped high into the
air over Obi-Wan. Obi-Wan's lightsaber swept out at
his attacker, swiftly severing Anakin's left arm above
the elbow and both legs at the knees.

Anakin shouted and lost his grip on his lightsaber as
his maimed body crashed upon black, smoldering sand

and tumbled down the slope. Obi-Wan watched in horror as Anakin came to a rest near the edge of the lava river, and lifted his head to face his former friend and Master. Anakin's eyes were filled with inhuman rage.

"You were the Chosen One!" Obi-Wan shouted.

Anakin retained his prosthetic right arm, and as he struggled to pull himself away from the lava, his eyes continued to blaze with fury at Obi-Wan.

"It was said you would destroy the Sith, not join them!" Obi-Wan continued. "Bring balance to the Force, not leave it in darkness!" Unable to look at his former apprentice, he turned away. He spied Anakin's fallen lightsaber, and bent down to pick it up before he turned to look at Anakin again.

"I hate you!" Anakin roared.

Obi-Wan stood in silence, stunned as he faced the seething, ruined remains of Anakin. "You were my brother, Anakin," Obi-Wan said, "I loved you."

Anakin's clothes caught fire, and he screamed as he was suddenly engulfed in flames.

For a moment, Obi-Wan hesitated. *He's gone*, Obi-Wan thought. *Anakin is gone.*

Obi-Wan finally turned away.

Anakin kept screaming.

As Obi-Wan staggered back to Padmé's starship, he was greeted by two droids: R2-D2, who had arrived on Mustafar with Anakin, and Anakin's gleaming, gold-plated protocol droid C-3PO, who had accompanied Padmé from Coruscant.

"Oh, Master Kenobi," C-3PO said as he came down the ship's landing ramp. "Um, we have Miss Padmé on board."

As Obi-Wan quickened his step, C-3PO continued, "Yes. Please, please hurry. We should leave this dreadful place."

Obi-Wan was very concerned about Padmé because he knew she was pregnant. He also knew that Anakin was the father.

Leaving Mustafar, Obi-Wan and the droids brought Padmé to a research base in the Polis Massa asteroid system, where Obi-Wan and Bail Organa were waiting for them. Padmé was unconscious, and Obi-Wan carried her directly to the base's medical center.

A medical droid delivered the terrible news in a flat voice. Padmé was dying. She had lost the will to live. The droid added that they would have to operate quickly to save Padmé's babies — Padmé was carrying twins.

Obi-Wan was in the operating room for the delivery of Padmé's babies. She named her son Luke and her daughter Leia.

As Obi-Wan held Luke in his arms, Padmé beckoned, "Obi-Wan?" He met her gaze, and she said, "There's good in him." She gasped, then continued, "I know. I know there's . . . still —"

And then Padmé Amidala died.

Obi-Wan just stood there for a moment, holding the baby boy in stunned silence. He had felt so utterly powerless as Padmé breathed her last, and not just because he couldn't stop her from dying. Even though he believed that there wasn't a trace of goodness left in Anakin, he also knew that it would have been a kindness on his part if he had somehow assured the dying woman that he shared her conviction. All it would have taken on his part was a smile or a slight nod, and she might have died in peace. But in the end, he had been powerless to even manage that.

Leaving Polis Massa on Bail Organa's consular starship, *Tantive IV*, the group transported Padmé's body back to Naboo. While Organa's aides attended to Padmé's newborn babies, Obi-Wan met with Yoda and Bail in the *Tantive IV* conference room to discuss the fates of Luke and Leia.

Yoda sat at the head of a long table, with Obi-Wan seated to his left and Bail to his right. Yoda said, "Hidden, safe, the children must be kept."

Obi-Wan agreed. "We must take them somewhere where the Sith will not sense their presence."

"Hmm," Yoda murmered. "Split up they should be."

"My wife and I will take the girl," Bail volunteered. "We've always talked of adopting a baby girl. She will be loved with us."

"And what of the boy?" Obi-Wan asked.

"To Tatooine," Yoda said. "To his family send him."

Obi-Wan considered this, then said, "I will take the child and watch over him."

Bail and Obi-Wan exchanged glances, then rose from their seats. Yoda said, "Until the time is right, disappear we will."

Bail exited the conference room. Obi-Wan was about to leave, too, when Yoda said, "Master Kenobi, wait a moment." The elderly Jedi gestured for Obi-Wan to return to his seat, then continued, "In your solitude on Tatooine, training I have for you."

Not sure that he had heard correctly, Obi-Wan said, "Training?"

"An old friend has learned the path to immortality," Yoda said. "One who has returned from the netherworld of the Force. Your old Master."

Astonished, Obi-Wan gasped, "Qui-Gon?"

"How to commune with him, I will teach you."

R2-D2 had been to the Lars family moisture farm just prior to the Battle of Geonosis, and was able to provide the farm's coordinates to Obi-Wan. The starfighter that Obi-Wan had taken from the late General Grievous had remained in *Tantive IV*'s docking bay, and Obi-Wan planned to use the starfighter to take Luke to a spaceport at Nar Shaddaa, a moon in a space sector controlled by the Hutts. As Obi-Wan carried Luke into the starfighter's cockpit, R2-D2 beeped a farewell message to the Jedi. There was no point in Obi-Wan saying good-bye to C-3PO, for Bail Organa had already taken the security precaution of having the talkative protocol droid's memory erased.

Holding Luke Skywalker's swaddled form against his chest, Obi-Wan Kenobi sat in an uncomfortable seat on a crowded, Tatooine-bound starcruiser. The Jedi Master had little experience holding babies, but he did his best to look comfortable with the child in his arms.

Bail Organa had provided a supply of untraceable credits for Obi-Wan to pay for the journey to the sand planet. To further maintain secrecy, Obi-Wan and Luke were traveling to Tatooine via an indirect route starting from Nar Shaddaa on a series of public transports. During a layover at a space station, Obi-Wan witnessed a group of travelers at a HoloNet kiosk, watching a broadcast about recent events on Coruscant. Obi-Wan had cringed when he saw a hologram of Emperor Palpatine urging viewers to report anyone whom they suspected of being a Jedi or having "supernatural powers." Palpatine's words had prompted one traveler to remark, "Thank goodness those terrible Jedi were stopped!"

Obi-Wan had remained silent and kept his head low as he carried Luke. The Tatooine-bound starcruiser had been delayed, but he did everything he could to keep the baby comfortable. Unfortunately, the final flight turned out to be a nightmare. Most of the other passengers were either Podracers or obnoxious Podrace enthusiasts. Even more distressing, Obi-Wan was running low on the baby food supplements and sanitation material that the Polis Massans had provided. All in all, he was beginning to wonder if avoiding a more direct route had been a mistake.

Luke made a burbling sound. Obi-Wan patted the baby's back and said in a soothing tone, "Easy, young one. Easy now."

One of the Podracers, a nimble-handed Dug with goggles on his head, was exercising his arms by walking back and forth across the headrests on the seats in front of Obi-Wan. Without breaking his stride, the Dug turned to someone seated up ahead of him and shouted, "Hey, Bumpy! Your nose still hurtin' since the last time you punched Ben's Mesa?!" Then the Dug broke out into a wheezing laugh.

Keeping his eyes on the Dug, Obi-Wan shifted his arm around Luke to a more protective position and thought, *If that clown falls on top of us, so help me, he'll know what a punch feels like.*

Several seats ahead, a Nuknog — presumably "Bumpy" — jumped up and hurled an unopened bottled beverage at the Dug. The Dug saw the incoming bottle and jerked his body to the side to avoid getting hit, allowing the bottle to arc past his body and fall straight toward Luke.

Just as the Dug rapidly turned his pronounced snout around to see where the bottle would strike, Obi-Wan's right hand flew up and away from Luke to catch the bottle in midair. Obi-Wan held the bottle out to the Dug and said tersely, "I believe this was meant for you."

The Dug just looked at Obi-Wan for a moment, before muttering a half-hearted "Thanks." He took the bottle, opened it with his teeth, and then turned and whipped the bottlecap back at his would-be attacker. Returning his attention to Obi-Wan, he said, "You move fast for a human."

Obi-Wan felt a chill travel down his spine. *Oh, no.*

The Dug's mouth twisted back into a vicious leer, "In fact," the Dug continued, "the only kind of humans I've ever heard of that can move that fast are —"

"Aren't you tired?" Obi-Wan interrupted, his gaze riveted to the Dug's eyes.

The Dug blinked, and his eyelids became suddenly heavy. He looked at his bottle, and then back to Obi-Wan. "Now that you mention it," the Dug said with a wide yawn, "I *am* tired."

"Forget you ever saw me, and take a long nap."

"I didn't see anybody," the Dug muttered as his eyes closed. And then he fell backward, spilling the remaining contents of his bottle as his slumbering form tumbled onto the passengers seated in front of Obi-Wan.

Obi-Wan silently cursed himself. He couldn't have let the thrown bottle hit Luke, but his Jedi reflexes had nearly given him away. *Just one wrong move*, he thought. *All it takes is one wrong move.*

Luke wiggled against his chest.

I must be more careful.

Obi-Wan pulled his cloak down lower over his face. Except for a few soothing words to Luke, he spoke with no one else for the remainder of the flight.

The data provided by R2-D2 allowed Obi-Wan to find the Lars Homestead without difficulty. Obi-Wan was glad and relieved that Beru and Owen agreed to raise Luke, but his mission did not end there, as it was also his duty to watch over the boy. He had thought that his ongoing presence would be some comfort to Owen and Beru.

He soon learned that he was mistaken.

CHAPTER SEVEN

Not long after delivering Luke to Owen and Beru, Obi-Wan was riding his eopie east across the desert. He had acquired the eopie just after his arrival to Tatooine, when he needed a method of transport to deliver Luke to the Lars homestead, and the beast had continued to prove itself useful. It was while riding the eopie that he had found shelter for himself, a small hovel — at least it had a secure door — that had been carved out of a nearby canyon wall before it was abandoned by some unknown transient. The eopie also allowed him to check on the Lars homestead twice daily, at sunrise and sunset, which had become his routine.

Whenever he rode, he was always mindful of his surroundings and on the lookout for danger. He had already seen various signs of Tusken Raiders, and was fairly certain that at least one Tusken tribe had become aware of his presence.

Recently, while exploring the vast area around the Lars homestead, he had come upon what appeared to be the ruins of a camp in a canyon in the Jundland Wastes. He had traveled close enough to the ruins to see a cluster of bantha-rib arches sticking in the sand, all that remained of several small huts, the kind used by the nomadic Tuskens. Seeing the ruins, Obi-Wan had been suddenly overcome by a feeling of loneliness and despair, which ended a moment later, when a distant, blood-chilling howl echoed down from a nearby clifftop. Suspecting that he may have strayed into an area that was somehow sacred to Tuskens, he had proceeded past the ruins quickly.

Sometimes while riding, his thoughts would stray to Padmé on her deathbed. Speaking of Anakin, her last words had been, "There's still good in him."

And then he would think of how he had left Anakin to die on Mustafar.

He tried to suppress such thoughts. The problem was Obi-Wan remembered so many good years with Anakin, and really had loved him like a brother. It was still so hard for him to believe that Anakin had turned to evil. And even after all the unforgivable things he had done under the name of Darth Vader, Obi-Wan still found himself missing his friend Anakin Skywalker.

He also thought of Qui-Gon Jinn. Yoda had explained to Obi-Wan that Qui-Gon's consciousness had survived as a spiritual entity, and described his own exchanges with

Qui-Gon's disembodied voice. Yoda had also instructed Obi-Wan how to communicate with Qui-Gon, but so far, Obi-Wan had yet to hear from his Master's spirit.

The suns had almost set as he approached the perimeter of the Lars homestead. As usual, the security lights were already switched on and a few KPR servant droids were patrolling the area around the underground compound. On previous evenings, Owen had emerged from the entrance dome to check the droids before returning below ground for the night. Obi-Wan had come to interpret Owen's action as a signal that all was well, and that it was time for him to make his way back to his hovel. But on this night, Obi-Wan found Owen standing several meters away from the entry dome, carrying a blaster rifle, and waiting for him.

Owen held the blaster rifle so it was aimed at the ground. Obi-Wan wasn't surprised to see the weapon, as Owen always carried it when he stepped outside at nightfall. But even without Jedi powers, Obi-Wan could see the man looked jittery.

"Hello, Owen," Obi-Wan said as he brought the eopie to a halt. "Is something wrong?"

Owen nodded once. Obi-Wan began to dismount, but Owen held up one hand and said, "Don't bother. What I have to say won't take long."

Obi-Wan kept his eyes on Owen as he shifted his weight back onto the eopie.

"I'm not sure how to put this," Owen continued, "so I'm just going to say it. The way you come around my place . . . it bothers me."

Obi-Wan sighed. "I'm sorry, Owen. But as I told you, I need to make sure that the boy is —"

"Wait," Owen interrupted. "My wife and I are the ones raising Luke, right? That's what we agreed to?"

Obi-Wan nodded as he wondered where the conversation was going.

Owen said, "Well, I *didn't* agree to you checking on us daily, let alone twice a day. I don't mean any disrespect, but I've been keeping Tuskens off my property for years, and . . . well, I think you coming here so often is just a bad idea!"

Keeping his voice calm, Obi-Wan said, "Owen, I assure you, I don't question your ability to handle the Tuskens. But as we've already discussed, it's not the Tuskens I'm worried about."

"Oh, right," Owen said. "It's the *Empire*. But then let me ask you something." Owen swallowed hard before he continued. "If you're so concerned about the child's well being, why don't you try staying away from us? Didn't you ever think what would happen to Luke if the Empire tracked you down and found you living in my backyard?"

Owen's words left Obi-Wan momentarily dumbstruck. Then he shook his head and said, "Forgive me,

Owen. You're absolutely right. I'll be more careful. More discreet."

"That's a start," Owen said. "Again, I don't mean any disrespect, but . . . my wife and I can't raise Luke in any ordinary way if we know you're always lurking about. Understand?"

"Yes," Obi-Wan said. He expected — maybe even hoped — that Owen was going to say something more, but when he didn't, Obi-Wan said, "Good night, Owen."

Owen nodded once again, then turned and headed for the entry dome. Obi-Wan turned his eopie around and guided the creature back across the desert.

Obi-Wan continued to monitor Luke, but from greater distances and without any obvious routine. He had no reason to remain in the hovel near the Lars homestead, so like the transient who had lived there previously, Obi-Wan moved on.

He eventually found a slightly more spacious derelict structure in the Jundland Wastes, a small, domed-roofed hut that sat on a bluff at the southwestern edge of the Dune Sea. Like so many other buildings on Tatooine, it was made of synstone, a mixture of crushed local rock and dissolvants that could be cast into almost any shape. The hut was approximately 136 kilometers from the Lars homestead — farther than Obi-Wan would have preferred, but probably still too close to satisfy Owen Lars. From what Obi-Wan could see, no one had lived in the hut for a very long time. An old moisture vaporator stood beside it. Obi-Wan checked to see if the vaporator worked. It didn't.

To confirm whether the hut was indeed abandoned, Obi-Wan traveled to the property bureau in Tatooine's capitol city, Bestine. Inside the bureau, on the wall beside the information desk, there was a holographic map of Tatooine. Obi-Wan's eyes happened to fall on a broad, flat-topped mountain that the map identified as *Ben's Mesa.*

That sounds familiar, Obi-Wan thought. Then he recalled the loudmouth Dug who had been on the same flight that had brought him to the sand planet.

An antique, oval-faced droid clerk wobbled up behind the information desk, looked at Obi-Wan through tarnished photoreceptors and said, "May I help you, Mister —"

"Ben," Obi-Wan replied flatly. "I'm interested in a piece of property. The location coordinates are Alpha-1733-Mu-9033."

The droid clerk turned his photoreceptors to a data-bank monitor and entered the coordinates. A moment later, he replied, "There are no filed claims or liens for the property at Alpha-1733-Mu-9033, Mr. Ben."

Not sure he understood, Obi-Wan said, "In other words, the place is available?"

"No one lives there," the droid answered curtly.

"No one *wants* to live in the Jundland Wastes." But then the droid's head made a clicking sound as it evaluated the situation, and added, "Do you want to file a claim, sir?"

Obi-Wan considered making a claim under an assumed name, but then decided against it, knowing that he had a better chance of maintaining a secret presence on Tatooine if he stayed off of any official records. "No, thanks," Obi-Wan said as he moved toward the exit. "I think the property should remain as it is."

"As you wish, sir," said the droid, not really caring one way or the other.

Obi-Wan's next stop was a hardware shop, where he used most of his remaining credits to buy all the tools and supplies that he could afford and his eopie could carry.

Excluding the hovel he had lived in during his first weeks on Tatooine, Obi-Wan had never inhabited a place by himself for any great duration. Like most Jedi, he had lived much of his life at the Jedi Temple on Coruscant. Now, living in an area on a world where even the most basic supplies were difficult to obtain, he was hardly prepared for the work required to restore the abandoned hut. But while he monitored Luke over the months that followed, he also threw himself into making the hut as livable as possible. He had no idea how long he might reside on Tatooine, but he wouldn't be a very useful Jedi if the roof over his head came crashing down on him.

There was a surprising amount of wildlife in the Jundland Wastes. By watching various creatures, including his own eopie, Obi-Wan learned where to gather berries and vegetables. By watching womp rats and other omnivores, he also determined which animals were edible. His Jedi reflexes enabled him to catch the fast-running, two-legged rodents called scurriers as easily as most people could pull an amphibious gorg from its primal root puddle. But if he had to choose, he preferred the taste of gorgs.

For all of Obi-Wan's self-sufficient achievements, there were some things he simply couldn't do on his own. He required special tools and materials to fix and clean the moisture vaporator beside the hut, the stove in his living area, and the water cistern in the cellar. He was fortunate that a passing clan of Jawa traders took notice of him one day and parked their massive sand-crawler near his hut. Evidently, the maroon-cloaked creatures had become aware of the strange man who had moved to the Jundland Wastes, and were impressed by the fact that he had survived as long as he had. The Jawas were happy to share their tools and some spare supplies with Obi-Wan, especially after he offered to share some food with them.

Obi-Wan further gained favor with this clan after he noticed three young Jawas had taken a liking to his eopie, which he encouraged them to take as a gift from him. The Jawa leader responded by chittering and gesturing at the sandcrawler to convey that he would be happy to give Obi-Wan rides to the cities or settlements, which was exactly what the Jedi had hoped he would do. After all, Obi-Wan no longer required an eopie on a daily basis, and sandcrawlers traveled faster.

"Thank you, my friend," Obi-Wan answered the Jawa chief. "I just might take you up on that offer. Please, call me Ben."

Not long after befriending the Jawas, Obi-Wan rode with them to Anchorhead, a wind-scoured settlement about twenty kilometers east of the Lars homestead. Anchorhead was a small community and trading post, with about a dozen pourstone stores and two small cantinas. One of the larger buildings was Tosche Station, which supplied energy to most of the area moisture farms. Obi-Wan had told the Jawas that he was in search of either parts or a replacement for his hut's moisture vaporator, as he still hadn't managed to get it working properly, but he had another reason for making the journey. Using the Force, he had anticipated that Luke was heading into Anchorhead with his aunt and uncle.

Obi-Wan was in one of the cantinas, The Weary Traveler, having a drink of water as he watched Owen, Beru, and Luke. They were at the provisions store across the street from the cantina. Beru was carrying Luke in a sling that she wore over her chest. Obi-Wan had been careful to position himself so the Lars family would not see him. He was glad to see they all looked healthy and happy.

The cantina had an old hyperwave repeater that was broadcasting intermittent HoloNet displays of recent news reports from across the galaxy. Obi-Wan was looking at Luke when he thought he heard a female HoloNet reporter say the word "Jedi."

Obi-Wan looked to the cantina's HoloNet display, but a sudden burst of static interrupted the broadcast. He turned to human man seated two tables away and said, "What was she saying?"

"Band of Jedi were killed on Kashyyyk," the man replied.

Oh, no, Obi-Wan thought.

The broadcast resumed. The Empire claimed Kashyyyk had been plotting a rebellion. Imperial forces not only killed the unidentified Jedi but also thousands of Wookiees. Hundreds of thousands more Wookiees had been imprisoned.

Obi-Wan's mind reeled as he thought of the slain Jedi. *What were they thinking? They should have gone into hiding, not drawn attention to themselves! Couldn't they foresee what would happen to the Wookiees?*

The HoloNet display squawked and flickered again, then displayed an image of a dark figure, someone clad in black armor from head to toe. Although the audio transmission was garbled, the images conveyed that this armored being or thing played a major role hunting down and executing the Jedi.

Then Obi-Wan heard the reporter say the name *Darth Vader.*

A few minutes and another glass of water later, Obi-Wan picked up his rucksack and staggered out of the cantina. Although he had not forgotten that he had come to Anchorhead to check on Luke, his mind was no longer focused on staying out of sight from Owen Lars. His thoughts were on Vader.

He couldn't believe it. Somehow, Anakin had survived the duel on Mustafar, and had resumed his Sith title of Darth Vader. Obi-Wan had concealed his lightsaber beneath his robes, and as he walked along Anchorhead's main street, his right hand's fingers wrapped around the weapon protectively.

Did I drive Anakin deeper into the dark side by abandoning him on Mustafar?

Could I face Anakin again?

If I did, could I kill him?

Across the street, he saw Beru, carrying Luke as she walked beside Owen, moving from one store to the next. Fortunately, there were a few dozen other people walking about, and Owen and Beru were still unaware of Obi-Wan's presence. But as Obi-Wan's eyes locked onto the Lars family, the Jedi felt more uneasy than ever.

Should I warn them about Vader? Should I take Luke away from them? Hide him away on an even more remote world?

Obi-Wan had been trained to be fearless. But as he thought of Luke's safety, he was almost overwhelmed by the anxiety that swept over him. And then, from out of nowhere, he heard a disembodied voice — sounding not through his ears, but directly into his thoughts — that caused him to stop in his tracks.

"Obi-Wan."

Recognizing the voice immediately, Obi-Wan stopped in his tracks. "Qui-Gon! Master!"

Obi-Wan was suddenly, acutely aware that anyone on the street might think he was talking to himself. Not wanting to be branded as a lunatic, he quickly moved into an alley between two stores. Although he had many questions for Qui-Gon, the HoloNet broadcast prompted him to first ask, "Master, is Darth Vader Anakin?"

"Yes," Qui-Gon's voice replied. "Although the Anakin you and I knew is imprisoned by the dark side."

Standing in the alley, Obi-Wan scowled. "I was wrong to leave him on Mustafar. I should have made *sure* he was dead."

"The Force will determine Anakin's future. Obi-Wan: Luke must not be told that Vader is his father until the time is right."

"Should I take further steps to hide Luke?"

"The core of Anakin that resides in Vader grasps

that Tatooine is the source of nearly everything that causes him pain. Vader will never set foot on Tatooine, if only out of fear of reawakening Anakin."

Genuinely relieved to hear this, Obi-Wan said, "Then my obligation is unchanged. But from what Yoda told me, I know that I have much to learn, Master."

"You were always that way, Obi-Wan," Qui-Gon said, his words unexpectedly fading out. But Obi-Wan knew they would speak again.

Though he was not fearful anymore, Obi-Wan stayed to watch over Luke, Beru, and Owen for a while longer, until it was time for them to return to their respective homes.

The next time Obi-Wan visited Anchorhead to obtain supplies, he found an unusual rectangular-shaped item in a junk shop. The shopkeeper was apparently unfamiliar with the item's function, and was using it as a shelf to display a small selection of used power couplings. But Obi-Wan — now known locally as Ben — recalled handling similar objects in the collection of the Jedi Archives, and recognized the "shelf" as an ancient, leather-bound book.

Obi-Wan moved the power couplings aside and opened the book. Incredibly, only a few pages were slightly discolored, and all were blank. He had never considered writing a journal before, but suddenly realized that a journal would be a good way to preserve information about the Jedi.

Information that Luke might need someday.

Holding the book up for the shopkeeper to see, Obi-Wan said, "Do you know if this thing will burn properly?"

The shopkeeper shrugged. "Beats me what it's good for, Ben," he said. "But it's yours for a credit."

Ben did not haggle.

CHAPTER EIGHT

Ben Kenobi had been on Tatooine for nearly two years when he learned about an unusual increase of atrocities committed by Tusken Raiders. According to fragmented reports, the Tuskens had attacked three moisture farms and left seven colonists dead in a single day. But what disturbed Kenobi even more than the killings was the unnerving disturbance in the Force that came with them. It was as if a dark presence had touched upon the desert world, creating an almost tangible trace of evil in the air.

Could it be the Sith? Ben didn't know. All he could do was keep a closer eye on Luke.

Leaving his home in the Jundland Wastes, he found a bantha that had strayed from its herd. Because taming such beasts was a simple task for a Jedi Master, Ben was soon riding the bantha, heading southwest. He had intended to travel directly to the Lars homestead, but was just a few kilometers into his journey when he neared the ruins of the Tusken camp—the same one he had discovered not long after his arrival on Tatooine, from the back of his old eopie—and he came to a stop.

The camp ruins always emanated a dreadful feeling whenever Ben traveled near it, and he had never felt compelled to inspect it more closely. On this particular day, the feeling was worse, practically sickening, and yet Ben sensed that the place was somehow beckoning him. He tried to urge the bantha forward, but the bantha took only two cautious steps before it came to a halt, then snorted at the sand and refused to budge.

Because the Tuskens had used bantha ribs as supports for their huts, Ben could hardly blame his mount for wanting to keep her distance from the ruins. He dismounted, leaving the bantha as he walked closer to the ruins.

Amidst the remnants of one hut, he noticed a bantha rib arch with dark spatters on it, the kind of spatters only blood could make. Then he saw two rawhide strips that dangled from the arched ribs. Noting the height and position of the rawhide strips, Ben knew immediately that they had been used to secure a captive human's outstretched arms.

And then it hit him.

This is where Anakin's mother died.

Ben didn't just sense it, he knew it for a fact. For a moment, he resisted the urge to tear his eyes from the rawhide strips because he feared that if he looked away,

119

the ruins might disappear along with the knowledge that came with them. When he did finally pry his gaze from the bloodstained arch, he saw the numerous bones that poked up through the sand around and throughout the ruins, bones that were much too small to have come from banthas. Shmi Skywalker had not died alone.

Ben did not have to guess who had slaughtered the Tuskens.

"Now you know," said Qui-Gon Jinn's disembodied voice.

Ben was still so stunned that he didn't even slightly flinch when he heard Qui-Gon, whose voice sounded as if it came from above and behind Ben's head. Ben said, "Why didn't you tell me about this?"

"You weren't ready," Qui-Gon said. "You're *still* not ready."

"Not ready?" Ben echoed. He swallowed hard before he continued, "Master, if you mean that I'm not ready to understand what happened here, then I believe you're mistaken. Anakin killed an entire tribe of Tuskens out of vengeance, and then kept it a secret from everyone. Apparently, you were aware of this, and yet you *still* maintain he is the Chosen One. What more is there to know?"

Qui-Gon answered, "That Anakin did not keep it a secret from *everyone*."

Ben sighed. "Of course. He would have told Padmé. And Palpatine. And I suspect that if he didn't actually tell Owen Lars, then Owen figured it out for himself. If Owen has the impression that Jedi are prone to murder in the name of revenge, that would certainly explain why he's so cautious of me." Ben returned his gaze to the leather strips.

"And why did Anakin keep his secret from you?"

Ben was about to reply, *Because he was afraid he'd be banished from the Jedi*, but instead he shook his head and said, "It doesn't matter whom Anakin told. What matters is that he was a Jedi, and that he became a butcher."

"You should not judge when you fail to understand."

Exasperated, Ben demanded, "Understand *what*, Master?"

"As I said, you're still not ready."

Ben sighed. "Well, when I am ready, I hope you'll let me know." He turned and began walking back to the waiting bantha.

"For now, Obi-Wan, know this," Qui-Gon said gravely, his voice sounding as if it were traveling alongside Ben. "Anakin revealed his secret to one other."

"Master, please," Ben said without breaking his stride. "If this is another guessing game, I don't think I —"

"A'Sharad Hett."

Ben stopped in his tracks. Since his arrival on Tatooine, he had thought of the Tusken Jedi on various occasions. He had assumed that Hett was among the many casualties of the Jedi purge. He said, "I don't believe you ever met A'Sharad Hett, Master."

"No," Qui-Gon replied, "I never did. But I did know his father. The Force was strong in the Hett family."

Glancing back at the ruins, Ben said, "The Tuskens that Anakin killed . . . were they Hett's tribe? Are you telling me that A'Sharad Hett is alive, that he's involved with the recent killings on Tatooine?"

"I cannot say," Qui-Gon answered vaguely.

Just then, a hot wind gusted across the ruins and swept over Ben. He was about to ask whether Qui-Gon was unable or unwilling to reveal certain details, but then his Master said, "May the Force be with you, Obi-Wan."

A moment after Qui-Gon's words trailed off with the wind, Ben turned away once again from the ruins. He climbed onto the bantha's back and rode off.

Ben rode the bantha all night. When he arrived at the outer perimeter of the Lars homestead, he released the bantha and continued on foot. As he walked past one of Owen's moisture vaporator towers, he saw a KPR droid peek out from behind the vaporator.

Ben ignored the droid. *Let Owen know I'm coming,* he thought. He suspected that Owen would rather see him than the Tuskens, at least.

He stopped half a kilometer from the domed entry to the Lars family's subterranean home, and pitched a low, sand-colored tent. He kept his cloaked body close to the ground, watching the horizon and listening for any rising dust or movement that might indicate incoming Tuskens.

Two days and nights passed. On the third morning, Ben finally saw someone approach. It was Owen Lars, walking straight toward him from the entry dome.

As usual, he was carrying a blaster rifle.

Rising up from the sand, Ben bowed his head and said, "Good afternoon, Mr. Lars."

Owen's rested the blaster rifle against his leg, the barrel pointed toward the ground. "I guess you heard about the recent attacks?"

Obi-Wan was slightly taken aback — he had expected Owen to immediately reprimand him for trespassing. Gesturing to his tent, Ben said, "That's why I'm here. Forgive me, Owen, I know you don't want me on your land. I tried to be discreet."

"Yeah, well, I've been keeping watch, too. And just so you know, I saw you arrive three days ago."

Ben was pleased that Owen had been monitoring the KPR droids, but he had the feeling that Owen wasn't in any mood to hear him say so. He noticed that Owen's eyes were somewhat bleary, probably from lack of sleep. Ben stayed quiet, waiting for Owen to continue.

Owen glanced back to his own home, then returned his gaze to Ben. "Normally, I'd tell you to get lost. But I just got word from a friend in Bestine. The Sand People attacked another farm." Owen looked away again. "Only one survivor," he continued. "A little girl. But she didn't last long."

Ben sighed. "I'm sorry, Owen."

"I'm not finished!" Owen roared, his eyes now blazing at Ben. The edge of Owen's upper lip quivered nervously.

He's not just angry, Ben realized. *He's terrified.*

Owen licked his lips before he continued. "The little girl . . . she said she saw one of the Sand People, maybe their chief. She said he . . . he used two 'laser swords.'"

Over the past three days since Ben's last exchange with Qui-Gon Jinn's spirit, Ben had had plenty of time to consider the possibility that A'Sharad Hett was involved in the recent killings. Still, hearing Owen's description of the marauder's leader made him feel suddenly queasy.

Oblivious to Ben's discomfort, Owen said through clenched teeth, "I don't suppose you've heard about any missing lightsabers on the planet, Mr. Jedi?"

"Get hold of yourself, Owen," he said, keeping his voice calm. "You know I had nothing to do with the attacks."

"Maybe not!" Owen said bitterly. "But I have some idea of what Jedi are capable of!"

124

"You're talking about Anakin," Ben said, "About what he did after he learned that his mother had been taken by Tuskens." It wasn't a question.

Owen winced, and then he scowled at the ground. "Shmi Skywalker was a good woman," he said. "We tried to rescue her, but my father…" The words caught in his throat, and he left the sentence unfinished. Tilting his chin in the direction of the entry dome, he continued, "When Anakin brought Shmi's body home, I'll never forget the look on his face. If killing me would have brought his mother back to life, I know he would have killed me then and there. I could see it in his eyes."

Ben grimaced. "Anakin never told me what really happened, Owen. Please trust that what he did that day was *not* the way of the Jedi."

"Well, I'm not so sure if that's a relief," Owen said. "Much as I didn't like the way he looked at me, I like the idea of Tuskens with lightsabers even less. There's not a person on Tatooine who wouldn't be happy if all the Tuskens were dead."

Ben offered no response. He knew that the deaths of Tuskens would not bring him any happiness, but he didn't believe there was any reason in explaining this to Owen.

Owen returned his gaze to Ben and said, "Look, I didn't mean anything bad against Jedi. I just figured you should know about this Sand Person out there, because maybe you're the only one who can stop him."

Owen looked away again. Ben thought, *He doesn't want to ask for my help. He's just too proud and stubborn.* "If it's all right with you," Ben said, "I'd like to stay close to your farm for a while. Just in case."

"Fine," Owen said flatly. He gestured to the nearest moisture vaporator and said, "If you need some water, help yourself." Then he turned and walked back to the domed entry to his home.

The Tusken Raiders arrived the next morning, at the strike of dawn. Instead of approaching from the east, which would have made them more difficult to see against the blinding, rising suns, they rode their banthas in from the west. Ben would have noticed them had they come from any direction across the desert, but he did briefly wonder why they chose their approach as they had. Then he dismissed the thought. *There's just no predicting Tuskens.*

Ben had moved closer to the moisture farm during the night. As the bantha-mounted Tuskens drew closer, they saw his cloaked form silhouetted against the sunrise. A breeze blew out from across the desert, and Ben's robes flapped against his body, revealing his lightsaber at his belt.

Most of the Tuskens were carrying *gaderffii*, long club-like weapons that some colonists referred to as "gaffi sticks." The Tusken on the lead bantha came to a stop a short distance away. The Tusken brayed in his native, guttural language to address his tribesman, then dismounted his bantha and walked slowly over to Ben. Attached to the Tusken's belt were two lightsabers. The moment Ben saw the weapons, the Tusken's identity was confirmed.

It was A'Sharad Hett.

Ben did not know whether Hett was aware that Anakin Skywalker had become Darth Vader. But if Hett knew—as Qui-Gon's spirit claimed—that Anakin was responsible for killing the Tuskens who tortured his mother, Ben could only imagine what Hett might do if he discovered the existence of Anakin Skywalker's son. Ben suspected that Hett knew nothing about Luke, if only because Luke was still alive. If Hett's sole purpose on Tatooine had been to kill Luke, Luke would probably be dead already. Now, as Hett approached, Ben banished all thoughts of Anakin and Luke from his mind.

Hett stopped in front of Ben, standing so close that Ben had to be careful not to inhale too deeply, for the stench of Hett's filthy robes and wrappings was almost overwhelming. Gazing into the red lenses of the Tusken's goggles, Ben said, "Master Hett."

"The Force be with you, Master Kenobi," replied Hett, his voice remarkably calm. "So, you too survived Order 66. I thought I was alone. What brings you to Tatooine, let alone these trackless wastes?"

"*You* do, Master Hett," Ben said without hesitation. Keeping his eyes fixed on Hett's goggles, he continued,

"You lead these Tuskens as their warlord. Not something a Jedi should do."

"Do not lecture me, Obi-Wan," Hett replied, still calm and without any hint of threat. "We were both generals in the Clone Wars, 'warlords' for a republic that turned on us." Hett shifted his feet slightly and turned to look past Ben and let his gaze travel across the moisture farm. "The Tuskens have been hunted and killed by both settlers and farmers. Jedi defend those who need help. Sometimes you defend life by taking the life of the aggressor."

"Past mistakes do not justify current ones," Ben said, not letting his eyes stray from Hett. "The danger is in becoming what you fight. It was the trap that the Jedi fell into. It is the trap that takes you now. It must stop. You *must* see that, A'Sharad Hett."

"I do not," Hett replied grimly. "I was raised to manhood amongst Tuskens by my father, Sharad Hett, the greatest Jedi of his age. He taught me to think and act as a Tusken." He remained facing the farm but gestured to the mounted Tuskens, and raised his voice as he said, "These are my people! Will the settlers stop killing Tuskens?"

Ben did not answer. He believed that the Tuskens could kill every settler on Tatooine and their hunger for violence would still be unsatisfied.

Taking Ben's silence as a negative response, Hett said, "Then blood calls for blood! The settlers will be forced to abandon the land . . . or be buried beneath it!"

"I cannot permit that," Ben said as he drew his lightsaber. "You were a great Jedi, Hett, and the son of a great Jedi, but you have given yourself over to revenge. It stops here." Ben ignited his lightsaber.

"You will have a Jedi funeral, Master Kenobi," Hett said. "That I promise."

Hett's hands dropped to his belt and the two lightsabers practically leapt into his gloved hands. He ignited both weapons at once, unleashing their identical green energy beams. He swung fast with the lightsaber in his right hand but Ben blocked it. The lightsabers sizzled loudly as they clashed.

It was fortunate for Ben that he had continued his Jedi exercises on Tatooine, that he had not allowed his reflexes to become dull. He did not think about how long it had been since he had last used his lightsaber in combat. Nor did consider that he was older than Hett by at least a decade, or Hett's considerable skills with his own weapons, and that the Tusken was far more experienced at fighting in the desert. Ben knew that any such thoughts would probably only get him killed.

As prepared as Ben was for many things, he was not ready to die. Not yet. Not today.

Hett brought his other lightsaber in at a sharp angle, forcing Ben to lurch back. Ben gripped his own weapon with both hands as he swung at Hett's legs, but Hett blocked the swipe. There was another loud sizzle as the blades dragged across each other.

Ben gasped as Hett launched a powerful kick to his midriff. The kick knocked Ben off his feet, and as he fell back through the air, Hett hurled one of his lightsabers at Ben's body. Ben clung tight to his own lightsaber as he twisted his body in midair to avoid being struck by the spinning blade of Hett's weapon. The moment Hett's lightsaber whipped past Ben's head, Hett used the Force to retrieve it, drawing it back to his waiting left hand.

As Hett caught the lightsaber, Ben rolled up from the ground and swung out again. Hett blocked the strike with his right lightsaber, then threw his left arm forward to smash his other lightsaber's handle into Ben's jaw.

Ben ignored the painful jolt to his head and reflexively brought his blade up high, forcing Hett to block the blow with his right lightsaber and leaving his own midsection briefly exposed. Before Hett could strike with his other lightsaber, Ben kicked him hard in the stomach.

Hett grunted, but he didn't go down. He lashed out again at Ben, kicking up sand as he moved in for the kill. Not one of the mounted Tuskens so much as flinched as they watched the duel, nor did they rally for their chief. They merely watched in silence, waiting for the outcome.

Ben blocked each blow, but he wasn't doing it with ease. Hett was far more experienced at fighting on the sand and in the desert heat. Ben knew that his opponent would never surrender, let alone withdraw. As much as he hoped to avoid killing Hett, he also knew that they couldn't keep fighting indefinitely.

But in the end, Ben knew he wasn't fighting for his own life. He was fighting for Luke's.

Quickly raising his left hand, Ben used the Force to push out at Hett, shoving him back through the air as Ben's lightsaber swept up and through Hett's right arm. Hett shouted as his arm fell away from his body. As Hett stumbled back, Ben used the Force to tear Hett's other lightsaber from his left hand's grip. Both of Hett's lightsabers deactivated as they sailed past Ben and landed in the sand behind him.

Hett crumpled to his knees. His tribesmen watched as Ben stepped forward, leaned down to grip the top of Hett's facemask, and then pulled the mask off his head.

The fallen Jedi cradled the wounded stump of his right arm as he lifted his gaze to meet Ben's. Hett's unmasked face was that of a human, but covered with black, angular tattoos.

Ben had no idea whether Hett's species or tattoos were an exception or the norm for Tuskens. Ben held the mask out before him, and then dropped it onto the sand in front of Hett's kneeling form.

Without a sound, the mounted Tuskens slowly turned their banthas around and began heading away from the moisture farm. Hett did not watch them depart, but continued staring at the sand in front of him. Ben, still wielding his activated lightsaber, remained standing near Hett, waiting for his next move.

"I am finished," Hett said, still averting his gaze. "You have disgraced me before my people. With one hand, I can no longer wield a gaderffii. I am now an outcast among the Tuskens." He said all this without a trace of emotion, and then added, "I am a dead man. Finish it. Kill me."

"No," Ben said as he deactivated his lightsaber. "But you can no longer stay on Tatooine. You must leave and give your word, by your father's honor, to never return."

Hett's brow furrowed.

Ben said, "Swear it."

Hett glowered, refusing to look at Ben, but then he finally muttered, "I so swear . . ."

Clipping his lightsaber to his belt, Ben said, "The Tuskens were once your people, but so were the Jedi. You have forgotten our ways. Perhaps, with meditation, you will remember them and yourself."

Hett offered no response.

"I hope you will," Ben said. "May the Force be with you, A'Sharad Hett." Then Ben turned and began walking toward the entry dome of the moisture farm. He was halfway to the dome when he glanced back to where he'd left the former Jedi, but Hett was already gone.

Owen Lars, still carrying his blaster rifle, was waiting for Ben in the doorway of the entry dome. Ben wondered if Owen had seen any of the vicious fight that had just occurred on his property. He hoped that he hadn't, and wasn't sure what to say. He just wanted to assure Owen that the Tuskens were gone. Before he could speak, Owen said, "It's over now, is it?"

"Yes," Ben said. The word almost cracked in his throat, and he suddenly realized just how thirsty he was.

"Well, then," Owen said. "You'd best be going." Then Owen turned and closed the door behind him.

Ben brushed the dust off his robe. After gathering his camp gear, he began the long walk back home.

He never saw A'Sharad Hett again.

CHAPTER NINE

Luke is in danger.

This awareness came suddenly and unexpectedly to Ben Kenobi. He had just stepped outside of his home and was carrying a compact toolkit to run a maintenance check on his moisture vaporator when the sensation hit him, a definite disturbance in the Force.

Ben froze in his tracks, stopping just shy of the vaporator. His grip automatically tightened on the toolkit's handle. He had been living on Tatooine for thirteen years, and although he had sensed disturbances in the Force before, he had never felt one quite like this.

Did Luke generate it? Ben wasn't sure. Luke was thirteen now. To the best of Ben's knowledge, the boy still knew nothing of the Force, but it was possible that Luke was unwittingly acting like a transmitter.

With his free hand, Ben reached up to pull his hood back, exposing his head to the blistering heat. A warm, steady wind gusted up from the desert floor, carrying with it dust and the distinct sound of an incoming Jawa sandcrawler that had not yet come into view.

Ben knew he had to stay calm. Taking a deep breath, he closed his eyes. He relaxed his mind, tuning out the noise of the sandcrawler's engine, and opening himself to the Force.

Almost immediately, he had a vision of flowing colors, a formless rush of tans and brown and . . .

Sandstorm!

. . . green . . . a dewback, running fast, leaving Luke and another boy behind it. Ben couldn't distinguish the other boy, but sensed he was one of Luke's friends . . . and not Biggs Darklighter.

An accident, Ben realized. *Caught in a sandstorm . . . the dewback tossed them . . .*

The boys were surrounded by high walls.

. . . in a canyon. Where?

Eyes still shut, Ben felt his feet shift beneath him, turning him until he stopped, facing southeast. He ignored the heat from the suns that bristled against the back of his neck. Seconds later, through closed eyes, he visualized a distinctive, jagged rock formation that loomed over the winding channels of a dried river bed.

Ja-Mero Ridge.

Ben sighed as he opened his eyes to gaze out across the Jundland Wastes. A hazy cloud was suspended over the area of Ja-Mero Ridge, just over seventy kilometers away. Because people had been known to lose their way in the twisted canyons even in clear weather, and because darkness would fall within a few hours, he knew that Luke and his friend might need help sooner than later.

Of all the times not to own a landspeeder!

Ben rapidly calculated how many hours it might take him to reach Ja-Mero Ridge if he traveled by foot, and checked his utility belt to make certain he carried adequate rations. As he walked around to the front of his house and placed the toolkit on the ground near the front door, it occurred to him that he might attempt to contact Owen Lars, but then immediately dismissed the idea. The Lars Homestead was easily another seventy kilometers *beyond* Ja-Mero Ridge, and Owen would just insist he didn't need Ben's help. *The stubborn fool would probably go searching for Luke and get himself lost or killed.*

Ben knew that both Owen and Beru would be worried sick if they had any idea of Luke's predicament, but there was nothing he could do about that now. Luke was in danger, and there was no time to waste. If he had any chance of finding the boys by nightfall, he would have to do it on his own.

Ben started walking away from his house. "Seventy kilometers," he muttered as he brushed the dust from his beard. "I don't suppose I'll have an easy time finding a taxi."

Just then, the Jawa sandcrawler came into view. The

mammoth vehicle was traveling west across the Xelric Draw, heading for Mos Espa.

"Ah," Ben said with a wry smile. "My taxi!"

The sandcrawler was moving fast, and Ben imagined the Jawas were eager to reach their destination. Reaching out with the Force, he visualized the chief Jawa on board the sandcrawler, and then projected a thought: *You should stop to check your engines.*

As if in response, the sandcrawler rumbled to a stop near the base of the bluff below Ben's house, and then several Jawas scurried out of the vehicle. Ben trudged down the bluff to meet the Jawas, who told him they had stopped to check their engines. Ben was not surprised that they found nothing wrong.

Ben conferred with the chief Jawa. A few minutes later, the sandcrawler pulled away from the bluff, carrying Ben with it. When the sandcrawler turned around to head into the Jundland Wastes, most of the Jawas were baffled by their change in course, but the chief Jawa insisted that it would be their pleasure to take Ben to Ja-Mero Ridge.

The wind was wailing when the sandcrawler came to a stop a short distance from the mouth of a narrow canyon. Ben climbed out, pulling his cloak up over his head to keep the stinging sand out of his face. As the sandcrawler turned around and drove away, Ben moved ahead, proceeding into the canyon.

As much as he looked forward to the day when he might meet Luke, he had no idea whether this would be that day. He had to allow the possibility that Luke and his friend could find their way out of the canyon without assistance, and saw no reason to reveal his presence to Luke unless it was absolutely necessary.

Ben kept moving. As he ventured deeper into the canyon, the air became noticeably colder. The sandstorm's gusts made it difficult to see more than a few meters in any direction. With the suns setting, he estimated total darkness in less than thirty minutes. He wondered just how well Luke was prepared to survive away from the Lars Homestead. *If he's as impulsive as his father, he'll think he's prepared for anything, even if he isn't*, he mused.

Some stones on the canyon floor had been recently disturbed, possibly kicked up by a large animal, maybe the dewback that Ben had visualized earlier. He followed the vanished animal's path until he met a fork in the canyon. Something in the air told him to take the left fork, which wound up leading him around a bend that brought him to another fork.

It's like a maze down here, Ben thought as he took the right fork, which was slightly wider than the other. Squinting his eyes, he glanced straight up and beyond the looming canyon walls, past the streaking gusts of sand, where a sliver of purple sky displayed a glimpse of a few dim stars. He didn't need to use the stars to get his bearings, but Luke might, as it would be easy for anyone to lose all sense of direction on the canyon floor.

Lowering his gaze, he continued into the encroaching darkness. Through the wind, he heard occasional sounds of creatures within canyon. None of them sounded threatening, but Ben had to concentrate to filter out the more distracting noises as he searched for the boys.

A small, unseen lizard, concealed within one of the many cracks in the wall to Ben's right, let out an anxious chirp. A moment later, Ben heard a swiftly approaching humming sound, and he ducked fast as several sketto whipped through the air. The four-winged, flying reptiles tore past him, angling back the way he had come until they vanished around a bend. Ben knew that the sketto normally stayed put during sandstorms, and he wondered what, if anything, had spooked them.

And then he heard a blood-curdling roar. Loud as thunder, it seemed to come from just around the next turn in the canyon. Ben recognized the cry instantly.

Krayt dragon!

His eyes went wide with alarm, but he was already moving, running as fast as he could around the turn. But when he emerged at another fork, where two ravines intersected, he stopped sharply. There was no sign of the beast.

An echo, he realized, at the same time sensing that Luke was still alive . . . *frightened,* but still alive. Ben almost cursed himself for not having discerned the roar as an echo before he went bounding into action like an overeager amateur. He stood frozen at the canyon's natural intersection, waiting for another sound to follow, and hoping that it wouldn't be human screams.

A moment later, there came a loud thud, something like a battering ram hitting a canyon wall. The crash reverberated down from the ravine at Ben's left. He ran into the ravine with his eyes forward, moving surely over and past jagged stones. As he ran, his nostrils flared slightly as he picked up the ugly scent of gored flesh, and then he almost ran straight into the source. It was a dewback's carcass.

Ben did not pause to examine the slaughtered dewback that practically filled the path before him. He scrambled over its body and kept running. He heard a steady thumping sound, but it was several strides later before he realized with some annoyance that the sound came from his own heart, which was pounding unusually fast. *Getting old,* he thought ruefully.

He focused on his heartbeat, slowing and stabilizing it as he ran on. The passage between the walls delivered Ben to the top of a ledge that overlooked a wider but still enclosed area. Looking into the gloom, he saw a krayt dragon — a canyon krayt, wild with hunger and rage — running straight for the mouth of a crevice. And inside the crevice were two cringing figures.

"Luke!" Ben shouted, without thinking or caring about whether he revealed his presence or awareness of Luke's identity. The dragon's massive horned head slammed into the crevice's outer wall, and stones exploded at the impact.

From inside the crevice, Luke's friend screamed, "We're dead!"

Not quite, Ben thought with immense relief, but then the krayt backed up and prepared to charge again. Using the Force, Ben reached out to the krayt dragon's primitive mind.

The monstrous beast suddenly stopped and roared, baring its long, yellowed teeth. Then it shook its wide head as if it were trying to shake something free, and snorted hard before it backed away from the crevice. Try as it might, and hungry as the krayt had been, it couldn't get rid of the thought that had suddenly entered its brain: it was tired. Very, very tired.

Sleep.

As gusts of sand continued to blast through the area, the krayt lowered its body onto the canyon floor, closed its eyes, and began to snore in great, long rasps.

Ben eased himself down from the ledge and stepped past the slumbering krayt to approach the crevice. As he neared the position of the two hiding boys, he heard Luke's friend whimper, "We're never going to find the way home! They'll find our bones one day . . . just old bones . . ."

Ben cleared his throat, and both boys jumped within the crevice as they turned their heads to face him. Both boys had sand goggles draped around their necks and were similarly attired in the faded white tunics and leggings that were typical of most moisture farmers. When Luke's eyes met his own, it suddenly occurred to Ben that Luke was the same age he had been when he made his first journey to Ilum.

Ben decided that this was, after all, the day he would finally introduce himself to Luke.

"I'm Ben Kenobi," he said. "We don't have much time if I'm going to get you boys home."

Luke gasped, "Do . . . do you know the way to the Lars homestead?"

Knowing that the less Luke knew of his purpose on Tatooine, the better, Ben appeared thoughtful and said, "Lars? Now, would that be Owen and Beru Lars?"

Luke nodded.

"It's been a very long time since I've seen them," Ben said, "but yes, I think I know the way."

He motioned for the boys to put their goggles on and follow him. Exiting the cramped crevice, they walked after Ben as he led them around the sleeping krayt. Although the boys had no idea where they were headed, they trusted Ben and kept up with him through the meandering turns in the canyon.

The winds began to die down as they exited the

canyon, and the night sky was mostly clear above the area where Ben had parted ways with the sandcrawler. Luke's young friend was apparently stunned by the abrupt change in weather, for he stammered, "What happened?"

"We're in the eye of the storm," Ben said, his eyes on the clouds that seemed to be churning against the horizon.

"If we keep a quick pace," Luke said, "we can travel with it long enough to find a safe shelter."

Luke's friend shook his head, and then sagged to his knees. Ben crouched down to examine the boy and confirmed that he was just exhausted. Lifting his gaze to Luke, Ben said, "I can carry your friend if you can keep pace, young man."

"Luke," Luke said. "Luke Skywalker."

Ben looked at him quizzically, wondering if the boy had heard when he'd called out his name in the canyon. If Luke had heard, he didn't mention it, but instead gestured to the other boy and said, "My friend is Windy Starkiller. We sure were lucky that krayt fell asleep when it did."

"Yes," Ben said as he lifted Windy up onto his back. "Lucky." Although he knew that luck had nothing to do with the krayt, he saw no point in telling Luke more than he needed to know. *He's not ready for the truth,* Ben thought. As he walked off with Windy on his back,

Luke at his side, and the stars above his head, his thoughts strayed to the dewback, who certainly hadn't been lucky that day.

Perhaps Luke won't ever be ready.

Ben glanced at Luke and saw his lower lip was trembling. "Something wrong, young Luke?"

"I was just thinking about our dewback," Luke replied. "He belonged to Windy, but we both took care of him. His name was Huey."

Ben found it interesting that he and Luke had been thinking of the dewback at the same time, but he stayed silent as he walked alongside Luke, waiting for the boy to continue.

"It's my fault he died," Luke said. "Windy and I were bored, and some of the older kids had been calling us 'small fry,' so . . . we decided to ride Huey out into the Wastes."

Ben nodded slightly to show that he was listening.

Luke said, "I got him killed because I wanted to prove that I wasn't a 'small fry.'" He kicked at the sand. "It was stupid coming out here alone, and Huey paid for it."

Adjusting Windy on his back, Ben replied, "My young friend, you have learned a valuable lesson about responsibility. Always keep this memory. Events in our lives have consequences that ripple through the lives of others."

Luke gave Ben a sidelong glance, and Ben realized

from the boy's somewhat baffled expression that his words may have overwhelmed the boy. Ben added, "All life is connected."

Luke seemed to think about this for a moment, then he nodded in agreement. Ben thought, *At least he listens.*

As Ben felt his back begin to ache from the strain of carrying Windy, the wind started to pick up again. Ben jutted his bearded chin toward a looming butte, which resembled a silhouette of an enormous tree stump against the dark storm clouds. "I know a safe place up ahead," Ben said. "We'll take shelter there."

While the winds wailed outside Ben's old hovel, Luke and a recovered Windy sat inside with Ben. Ben had secured the hovel's camouflage door, and the boys were happy to share the rations that he offered. After swallowing a nutrient tablet, Luke asked politely, "How long have you lived on Tatooine, Mr. Kenobi?"

Ben stroked his beard as he replied, "Longer than some, I suppose, but not as long as others."

"Oh," Luke said, apparently not noticing that Ben hadn't even slightly answered his question. Eager to learn more, Luke continued, "Do you have family here?"

Ben shook his head. "Just myself."

"Huh," Luke said. "I live with my aunt and uncle. Beru and Owen Lars. You said you know them?"

Knowing that Luke might relate their conversation to Owen, Ben said cautiously, "I recall whereabouts they live, but I regret I never really got to know them. Not well, anyway."

Luke's eyes brightened as he replied, "I'm sure they'll be happy to see you, especially after Windy and I tell them how you helped us."

That would be pleasant, Ben thought, but he doubted that Owen would ever be entirely happy to see him.

"My parents will want to thank you, too," Windy chimed in. Ben just smiled in return.

"If you don't mind my asking," Luke continued, "what were you doing out in the Jundland Wastes tonight?"

Ben said, "That's where I live."

Luke gaped. "You *live* in the Wastes?" He and Windy exchanged astonished glances, then Luke returned his gaze to Ben and added, "All by yourself?"

Ben gave a shrug, then said, "Well, a fellow has to live *somewhere.*"

"Don't you get ever get lonesome?"

"Not at all. As long as I have the suns in the morning and the moons at night, I'm reasonably content."

Windy said, "Do you live in a house, or a place like, um . . . ?" Moving his hands, he gestured at the hovel's interior.

Ben chuckled. "In fact, young Windy, I do live in a house."

Luke said, "Maybe we could visit you some time, Mr. Kenobi?"

"I'd enjoy that very much," Ben said. "But please, call me Ben."

"Sure . . . Ben."

"But before any of us go making more travel plans," Ben said, "let us try to get some rest. We can talk more in the morning."

Windy's worried parents were already at the Lars homestead, standing beside Owen and Beru, when Ben arrived with the two boys. Owen was clutching his blaster rifle. Windy ran straight to his mother who wrapped her arms around him.

"This is Mr. Kenobi!" Windy gasped. "He saved us from a krayt dragon!"

Windy's mother looked up to Ben and said, "Thank you, Mr. Kenobi!" Windy's father patted his son on the back as he smiled gratefully at Ben.

Ben returned the smile sheepishly, then looked to Owen. Owen glowered at him.

Luke arrived at Beru's side and exclaimed, "Mr. Kenobi told us stories about living out on the Dune Sea . . . it was great! Can he stay for a while?"

Without hesitation, Owen answered firmly, "Mr. Kenobi *has* to leave *now*."

There was a moment of awkward silence. Then Beru, clearly outraged, glared at her husband and said, "Owen Lars!"

Ignoring his wife, Owen stepped forward and

grabbed Ben's upper arm. "I want you off my property," Owen said, "and don't come back!" He gave Ben a shove.

Ben stumbled back but instantly regained his balance. Looking away from Owen, he faced Luke. Ben had hoped to talk more with Luke, who looked positively stunned by Owen's behavior. Now, all Ben could manage was a slight, sad smile for Luke before he turned and walked away.

Back home to the Jundland Wastes.

CHAPTER TEN

One day, during Ben Kenobi's nineteenth year on Tatooine, he felt an overwhelming urge to go for a walk in the canyons of the Jundland Wastes. As much as he enjoyed walking for exercise, he couldn't explain why he felt so compelled on this particular day, but decided to follow his instincts.

He was just a few kilometers from his home when he sensed danger in the canyon up ahead. More precisely, he sensed *Luke* was in danger.

What's that boy doing out here? Ben knew that Luke owned a skyhopper and had gained a local reputation as a talented pilot, but he also knew that Owen had recently grounded Luke after a reckless race at Beggar's Canyon. Before Ben could further ponder why Luke was so far from home, he smelled something in the air. *Tusken Raiders!* There was no mistaking their scent.

Ben pulled his cloak up over his head and quickened his pace. As he rounded a bend in the canyon, he saw three Tuskens rummaging through a landspeeder that was parked beside some large boulders. He recognized the speeder as Luke's, and then saw Luke himself lying motionless on the ground near the Tuskens. It appeared they had knocked him out cold.

Without breaking his stride across the canyon's stony floor, Ben performed his best imitation of a krayt dragon's hunting cry. The long, high-pitched howl echoed loudly off the canyon walls, prompting the Tuskens to grab their weapons and flee, leaving Luke and the landspeeder behind.

Ben moved swiftly beside Luke's unconscious form, bent down, and checked Luke's pulse. As he confirmed Luke was all right, he heard an electronic moan to his right, followed by a short beep. Ben paused, then pulled back his hood and turned to his right to see a blue-domed astromech droid cowering in the shadows under a rocky ledge.

Goodness, Ben thought. *It looks just like R2-D2.* He smiled at the droid and said, "Hello there!" Waggling his fingers in a beckoning gesture, he encouraged, "Come here, my little friend. Don't be afraid."

The droid emitted a series of concerned-sounding beeps.

"Oh, don't worry," Ben said as he gestured to Luke, "he'll be all right."

Luke stirred, then slowly opened his dazed eyes to look up at Ben. Ben helped him rise to a sitting position.

"Rest easy, son," Ben said, "you've had a busy day. You're fortunate to be all in one piece."

Luke rubbed the back of his head and then focused on his rescuer. "Ben?" he said. "Ben Kenobi? Boy, am I glad to see you!"

The astromech droid wobbled out from under the ledge and approached Luke and Ben.

"The Jundland Wastes are not to be traveled lightly," Ben said as he pulled Luke up to his feet. "Tell me, young Luke, what brings you out this far?"

"Oh, this little droid!" Luke said, gesturing at the astromech who beeped in response. Luke continued, "I think he's searching for his former master, but I've never seen such devotion in a droid before . . ."

Ben smiled again at the astromech, who beeped at him. Ben returned his gaze to Luke, who said, "Ah, he claims to be the property of an Obi-Wan Kenobi. Is he a relative of yours? Do you know who he's talking about?"

Ben's smile melted away. He kept his eyes on Luke and tried to remain calm, but the boy's words had practically stunned him. Catching his breath, Ben eased himself back to rest against a boulder. "*Obi-Wan* Kenobi . . ." he said. "Obi-Wan?" His gaze drifted to the ground. "Now that's a name I've not heard in a long time . . . a long time."

"I think my uncle knows him," Luke said. "He said he was dead . . ."

"Oh, he's not dead," Ben said, rolling his eyes with mild amusement. "Not yet."

"You know him?"

"Well, of course I know him. He's me!"

The astromech chirped as he rotated his dome to study Ben more closely.

Glancing at Luke, Ben said "I haven't gone by the name Obi-Wan since, oh, before you were born."

"Well, then, the droid *does* belong to you."

"Don't seem to remember ever owning a droid," Ben said, eyeing the blue astromech more carefully. As improbable as it seemed, he realized the droid *was* R2-D2. He recalled that R2-D2's counterpart, C-3PO, was supposed to have had a memory wipe, but he didn't know whether R2-D2 had undergone the same treatment, and thus wasn't certain if the droid even recognized him after so many years. *I've certainly aged more obviously than R2 has.* Ben kept his musings to himself, but muttered, "Very interesting . . ."

An inhuman braying sound echoed through the canyon. Ben looked up at the overhanging cliffs and said, "I think we better get indoors. The Sand People are easily startled, but they will soon be back. And in greater numbers."

Ben began moving toward the landspeeder and Luke followed, but then R2-D2 let out a pathetic beep, prompting Luke to exclaim, "C-3PO!"

What! Ben was astonished. *C-3PO is here, too?*

They found the protocol droid sprawled on some nearby rocks. Wires dangled out from the open socket at C-3PO's left shoulder, and his left arm lay on the ground a short distance away. Ben and Luke lifted the droid to a seated position.

In a dazed voice, C-3PO asked, "Where am I? I must have taken a bad step . . ." C-3PO turned his head from side to side, but when his photoreceptors saw Ben, he did not recognize the white-haired man.

"Well, can you stand?" Luke said. "We've got to get you out of here before the Sand People return."

"I don't think I can make it," C-3PO said. "You go on, Master Luke. There's no sense in you risking yourself on my account. I'm done for."

"No, you're not," Luke said sympathetically. "What kind of talk is that?"

Remembering the Tusken Raiders, Ben said, "Quickly . . . they're on the move."

Ben and Luke helped C-3PO to his feet, gathered up his left arm, and returned to the landspeeder. After they loaded the droids onto the vehicle, they sped off, heading out of the canyon and to the safety of Ben's house.

On the way back to the Ben's house, Luke explained how his uncle had bought the two droids from Jawa traders. After they arrived at the house, they went inside and Ben let Luke use his toolkit to repair C-3PO. Luke and C-3PO were seated on the couch beside a low round table across from Ben, who sat in a chair and watched as Luke quickly mended and reattached wires, and secured the droid's arm into place. R2-D2 stood near a storage chest on the floor and peered over the round table to watch the repair job.

The boy's as good at fixing things as his father was, Ben thought. Just then, R2-D2 beeped with what sounded like approval at Luke's technical skills, and Ben thought, *If you have any memory of Anakin, you're probably thinking the same thing.*

"Tell me, Luke," Ben said. "Do you know about your father's service in the Clone Wars?"

"No, my father didn't fight in the wars," Luke said as he reconnected another wire. "He was a navigator on a spice freighter."

"That's what your uncle told you," Ben said. "He didn't hold with your father's ideals. Thought he should have stayed here and not gotten involved."

Luke turned to face Ben. "You fought in the Clone Wars?"

"Yes. I was once a Jedi Knight, the same as your father," Ben said, easing back into his chair.

Luke looked away. "I wish I'd known him."

"He was the best starpilot in the galaxy and a cunning warrior." Ben paused and smiled at Luke. "I understand you've become quite a good pilot yourself."

Luke shrugged at this, but grinned sheepishly.

Ben smiled as he looked away. Remembering Anakin, he added, "And he was a good friend. Which reminds me . . ."

Ben pushed himself up from his seat and walked past R2-D2 to raise the lid on the storage chest. "I have something here for you." As he removed the shiny relic he had taken with him from the planet Mustafar, he said, "Your father wanted you to have this when you were old enough, but your uncle wouldn't allow it. He feared you might follow old Obi-Wan on some foolish idealistic crusade like your father did."

Still seated on the bed, C-3PO turned to Luke and said, "Sir, if you'll not be needing me, I'll close down for a while."

"Sure, go ahead," Luke said.

C-3PO remained seated as he switched himself off. His photoreceptors dimmed and his head slumped forward. Luke rose from the couch and stepped over beside Ben to see the object he had taken from the chest. Luke asked, "What is it?"

"Your father's lightsaber," Ben said, handing it to Luke. "This is the weapon of a Jedi Knight. Not as clumsy or random as a blaster."

Luke's fingers found the activation plate, and the lightsaber's blade blazed to life. He appeared fascinated as he tested the weapon, listening to its hum as he moved the blade back and forth through the air.

"An elegant weapon for a more civilized age," Ben commented as he returned to his chair. "For over a thousand generations the Jedi Knights were the guardians of peace and justice in the Old Republic. Before the dark times, before the Empire."

Luke deactivated the lightsaber and carried it with him as he sat back down on the edge of the bed. Facing Ben, he asked, "How did my father die?"

Ben glanced away from Luke. Choosing his words carefully, he returned his gaze to Luke and said gravely, "A young Jedi named Darth Vader, who was a pupil of mine until he turned to evil, helped the Empire hunt down and destroy the Jedi Knights. He betrayed and murdered your father."

Luke looked stunned.

"Now the Jedi are all but extinct," Ben continued. "Vader was seduced by the dark side of the Force."

"The Force?" Luke said.

"The Force is what gives the Jedi his power," Ben said. "It's an energy field created by all living things. It surrounds us and penetrates us. It binds the galaxy together."

R2-D2 beeped loudly, calling attention to himself.

Rising again, Ben stepped over to R2-D2 and said, "Now, let's see if we can't figure out what you are, my little friend. And where you come from."

As Ben touched R2-D2's dome, Luke said, "I saw part of the message he was —"

"I seem to have found it," Ben interrupted, for R2-D2's hologram projector had flicked on, causing a flickering hologram of a young, white-robed woman to appear atop Ben's round table. Ben returned to his seat.

"General Kenobi," said the woman's hologram, "years ago you served my father in the Clone Wars. Now he begs you to help him in his struggle against the Empire. I regret that I am unable to present my father's request to you in person, but my ship has fallen under attack, and I'm afraid my mission to bring you to Alderaan has failed. I have placed information vital to the survival of the Rebellion into the memory systems of this R2 unit."

Ben glanced at R2-D2, then back at the hologram.

"My father will know how to retrieve it," the woman's hologram continued. "You must see this droid safely delivered to him on Alderaan. This is our most desperate hour. Help me, Obi-Wan Kenobi. You're my only hope."

The woman's hologram glanced over her right shoulder, then bent as if she were adjusting something. Watching the hologram's movement, Ben suspected she must have turned in response to someone or something behind her before she bent to manually switch off R2-D2's holorecorder. The hologram flickered off.

Ben sat back in his chair and tugged at his beard, thinking hard. *The compulsion to walk to the canyon, the reunion with the droids and Luke, and now this message.* Obi-Wan did not believe in such things as coincidence. *It must be by the will of the Force.*

Luke said, "Who is she?"

On the subject of the hologram, Ben knew it was best to keep details to a minimum. He kept his expression impassive as he said, "She is Princess Leia Organa of the Royal House of Alderaan, an Imperial Senator and, unbeknownst to the Empire, a leader of the Rebel Alliance. She's grown into a remarkable young woman." Turning to Luke, he said, "You must learn the ways of the Force if you're to come with me to Alderaan."

"Alderaan?" Luke said with disbelief. Rising away from Ben, he added, "I'm not going to Alderaan." He moved toward the door, nervously shifting his lightsaber from one hand to the other. "I've got to get home. It's late. I'm in for it as it is."

"I need your help, Luke," Ben said. Nodding his head toward the table that had displayed the hologram, he added, "*She* needs your help. I'm getting too old for this sort of thing."

"I can't get involved!" Luke protested. "I've got work to do! It's not that I like the Empire . . . I hate it! But there's nothing I can do about it right now. It's such a long way from here."

"That's your uncle talking."

Luke sighed. "Oh, boy, my uncle," he said as he clutched the lightsaber tight with his right hand. Raising his left hand over R2-D2's domed head, he said, "How am I ever gonna explain this?" He brought his hand down on top of the droid's head with a slight *whack*.

"Learn about the Force, Luke."

Luke moved anxiously toward the door again, then stopped and turned to Ben. "Look, I can take you as far as Anchorhead," he said. "You can get a transport there to Mos Eisley or wherever you're going."

Ben looked away from Luke and said, "You must do what you feel is right, of course."

"What I feel is right?" Luke said, exasperated. "Ben, I'd like to help you, to help *her*, but is it right to run out on Uncle Owen and Aunt Beru? They're all the family I've got, and I'm not going to let anything happen to them! If that's not right, then maybe I'd rather be wrong!"

Ben nodded his head. "Yes . . . of course. Sometimes even the best intentions may be contradictory. Perhaps your answer lies with the Force, within you." Rising from his chair, Ben said briskly, "Very well, I shall take you up on your kind offer. I must make my way to Alderaan as quickly as I can."

Ben wondered if Luke would change his mind about leaving Tatooine by the time they reached Anchorhead, but he could not sense anything of the future. *Events are moving too fast*, Ben thought. *And today, the will of the Force is just too strong to resist.*

As Luke reactivated C-3PO, Ben discreetly secured his own lightsaber to his belt before donning his heavy robe. Suddenly, Ben realized that he might never return to his home in the desert, and that he had one thing left to do before leaving. Turning to Luke he said, "I think I might have an extra belt ring for your father's lightsaber. May I have the lightsaber for a moment so I can make sure the ring fits?"

"Oh, sure," Luke said, handing the lightsaber to Ben. "I'll load the droids onto the speeder and meet you outside."

As Luke and the droids headed out the door, Ben brought the lightsaber down into his cellar. He held the weapon carefully so he wouldn't smudge the fingerprints Luke had left on it. Moving quickly to his workbench, he used a small scanning device to record Luke's right thumbprint from the lightsaber, then transferred the print onto the access clasp for his journal. After placing the journal inside the boa-wood box, he transferred the same print onto the box's clasp. He set the scanning tool aside, and thought *That's that.* Remembering what he'd told Luke, he picked up a spare utility ring that he knew would fit the lightsaber. In less than two minutes, he was back upstairs and walking out the front door.

The droids and Luke were waiting for Ben at the landspeeder. As he climbed into the front seat beside Luke, he said, "Here you are," and returned the lightsaber along with the extra belt ring.

"Thanks!" Luke said as he took the lightsaber and

ring. Then he started the speeder and zoomed away from Ben's home, heading southeast.

Ben never looked back.

"I really do wish I could do more for you, Ben," Luke said as he guided the landspeeder along the edge of the Jundland Wastes. "But the sooner I get these droids out on the south ridge working on those vaporators, the less of a skinning I'll catch from Uncle Owen."

"Luke, I'm afraid the droids will have to come with me."

"What?" Luke exclaimed as he gave Ben a quick sidelong glance. "But they cost my uncle nearly —"

"Surely you don't think I can leave them behind?" Ben interrupted. "You heard that message. This matter is too vital to risk losing Artoo-Detoo, and for security's sake, See-Threepio must come along as well."

"But what'll I tell Uncle Owen?"

"I shall leave that to your conscience, son. But here's another thing to consider: There will almost certainly be Imperial agents seeking these two droids, people of the most violent and ruthless sort. Taking them back to your farm would only expose your uncle and aunt to dreadful danger."

"Oh," Luke said. "Oh, yeah. I'll . . . I'll think of something, I guess."

"Good," Ben said. "I know you will." Just then, he saw a rising smudge of darkness against the cliffs at the edge of the Wastes. He nudged Luke with his elbow as he pointed toward the cliffs and said, "Smoke!

"What?" Luke followed Ben's gaze. "Where? I don't see any . . . yes! There it is! You've got good eyes for . . . uh, I mean . . ."

". . . an old man?" Ben said with a grin. "Powers of observation lie with the mind, Luke, not the eyes. Perhaps we should take a look and see what it is."

Luke steered toward the fire, and they soon arrived beside what was left of a Jawa sandcrawler. Smoke billowed from fires that still burned inside and around the bulky, rusted vehicle. Dozens of Jawas lay dead, their small forms scattered across the sand.

At Ben's instruction, Luke stopped the landspeeder so they could examine the wreckage. The sandcrawler's hull was riddled with blaster-fire damage, and it appeared the entire Jawa clan had been wiped out.

"It looks like the Sand People did this, all right," Luke observed. Picking up a Tusken's weapon from the ground, he said, "Look, there's gaffi sticks, bantha tracks. It's just . . . I never heard of them hitting anything this big before."

"They didn't," Ben said. "But we are meant to think they did." Gesturing at the bantha tracks, he continued, "These tracks are side by side. Sand People always ride single file to hide their numbers."

Luke studied the small corpses that lay at his feet. "These are the same Jawas that sold us Artoo-Detoo and See-Threepio."

Ben pointed at the scorched dents in the sandcrawler's hull. "And these blast points, too accurate for Sand People. Only Imperial stormtroopers are so precise."

"But why would Imperial troops want to slaughter Jawas?"

Ben did not reply as Luke's gaze traveled to R2-D2 and C-3PO, who stood next to the parked speeder. Stepping toward Ben, Luke said, "If they traced the robots here, they may have learned who they sold them to, and that would lead them back . . . home!"

Luke bolted for the landspeeder.

"Wait, Luke!" Ben shouted. "It's too dangerous!"

Ignoring Ben, Luke jumped into the landspeeder, punched the ignition, and sped away from the burning sandcrawler.

When the speeder was no longer in sight, Ben turned to face the two droids. C-3PO said, "Where's Master Luke going, sir?"

"That I cannot tell you," Ben replied. "It's tied in with a great many things to be determined now by the Force."

C-3PO appeared nervous as he shifted from one foot to the other. R2-D2 emitted a low, whimpering whistle.

Ben surveyed the slain Jawas. "The poor little

creatures," he said. "Their lives were arduous and meager enough without being ended so brutally." Returning his gaze to the droids, he said, "We'll gather fuel and prepare a funeral pyre."

The suns were beginning to set and cast long shadows across the desert when Luke finally returned to the ruined sandcrawler. Ben watched Luke climb out of the speeder and walk past the droids. From Luke's anguished expression, Ben knew instantly that Owen and Beru were dead.

Ben's memory flashed to Anakin. Anakin had just turned twenty when he lost his mother on Tatooine, and now his nineteen-year-old son had lost his own surrogate parents on the same blasted planet. Recalling how Anakin had been transformed by his loss, and wondering if Luke might follow his father's path, Ben suppressed a shudder.

Eyes downcast, Luke staggered over to stand before Ben. Ben said, "There's nothing you could have done, Luke, had you been there. You'd have been killed, too, and the droids would now be in the hands of the Empire."

Luke lifted his gaze to Ben. "I want to come with you to Alderaan. There's nothing for me here now. I want to learn the ways of the Force and become a Jedi like my father."

Ben responded with a nod. He sensed Luke's sincerity, and hoped to teach him as much as he could. But then he thought again of Anakin . . . and Darth Vader. As much as he hoped Luke would become a Jedi, he was also determined to do everything in his power to make sure Luke would *not* become a Jedi like his father.

After the last Jawa had been placed on the pyre, the two men loaded the droids onto the landspeeder and drove off, heading east. Glancing up at the darkening sky, Luke said, "I'm afraid we won't reach Mos Eisley before dark."

Despite the urgency of their mission to Alderaan, Ben knew that both he and Luke required rest. The day had been extremely draining, mentally as well as physically. And because Imperial forces were now added to the list of perils on Tatooine, he also knew it was even more unwise to travel after sunset. He said, "We can be in Bestine soon enough. We'll find shelter there for the night."

CHAPTER ELEVEN

Leaving Bestine early the next morning, Ben, Luke, and the droids proceeded to Mos Eisley. On their way, Luke stopped his landspeeder on a high, craggy bluff that overlooked a wide canyon. The droids followed Luke and Ben to the edge of the bluff and gazed out over a wide, haphazard array of runways, landing pads, craterlike docking bays, and semi-domed structures that sprawled across the stark canyon floor.

"Mos Eisley spaceport," Ben said. "You will never find a more wretched hive of scum and villainy." Glancing at Luke, he added, "We must be cautious."

Ben and Luke got the droids onto the back of the landspeeder, and then the group resumed their journey.

Familiar with the route to Chalmun's Cantina on the far side of the city, Ben directed Luke through the dusty, busy streets of Mos Eisley Spaceport. Traffic consisted of not only landspeeders and swoop bikes but large quadrupeds, including dewbacks and long-necked rontos. While Ben was not surprised to see the wide variety of life-forms and transport that flowed past them, he realized with some amusement that Luke was trying hard not to gawk.

Approaching a congested intersection, Luke slowed the landspeeder to allow some pedestrians to pass. Suddenly, five white-armored stormtroopers emerged from the shadows of the buildings at the sides of the road. All carried blaster rifles. One stormtrooper — a squad leader with an orange pauldron over his right shoulder — waved at Luke, signaling him to pull over. Luke had driven straight into an Imperial checkpoint.

Ben noticed that the stormtroopers were looking at C-3PO and R2-D2, who were in plain view on the landspeeder's rear section. He glanced at Luke, who appeared extremely anxious as he clutched the speeder's steering wheel. Ben offered a reassuring smile to the boy, and then looked up at the squad leader who now loomed beside Luke's side of the speeder.

Facing Luke, the squad leader said, "How long have you had these droids?"

"About three or four seasons," Luke blurted out.

Keeping his eyes on the squad leader, Ben grinned affably and said, "They're up for sale if you want them."

Behind Luke, C-3PO trembled.

The squad leader said, "Let me see your identification."

In a calm, controlled tone, Ben said, "You don't need to see his identification."

The squad leader turned to his fellow stormtroopers and said, "We don't need to see his identification."

Ben said, "These aren't the droids you're looking for."

"These aren't the droids we're looking for," the squad leader repeated to the others.

Luke glanced at Ben, who gave him a slight, knowing nod. Ben returned his gaze to the squad leader and added, "He can go about his business."

The squad leader looked again to Luke and said, "You can go about your business."

"Move along," Ben said.

"Move along," echoed the squad leader, gesturing with his hand for Luke to proceed. "Move along."

Luke drove the landspeeder away from the checkpoint. Ben directed him along a curving street, and then they parked in front of Chalmun's Cantina. The moment the speeder stopped, a Jawa trotted over and ran his small hands over the vehicle's hood. C-3PO muttered, "I can't abide those Jawas. Disgusting creatures."

Ben and Luke climbed out of the landspeeder. "Go on, go on," Luke said as he shooed the Jawa away. While C-3PO helped R2-D2 off the back of the landspeeder, Luke turned to Ben. "I can't understand how we got by those troops. I thought we were dead."

"The Force can have a strong influence on the weak-minded."

Luke glanced at the cantina's run-down exterior. "Do you really think we're going to find a pilot here that'll take us to Alderaan?"

"Well, most of the best freighter pilots can be found here," Ben said. "Only watch your step. This place can be a little rough."

"I'm ready for anything," Luke said.

Ben led Luke and the droids into the cantina. Like many buildings in Mos Eisley, the cantina was essentially a hole in the ground that was covered by a domed roof. Its interior was dark, and the air was filled with thick smoke and fast music. Beyond the entry lobby, an arched doorway led to a short flight of mud-packed steps that descended into a crowded room. A disheveled, middle-aged man with hardened features stood behind the U-shaped bar that dominated the room's center, and the walls were lined by small booths that offered some slight possibility for private conversations. Most of the patrons were aliens, as were the Bith musicians who performed at the bandstand to the right of the bar.

While Luke stood gawking in the entry lobby with the droids behind him, Ben stepped down and made his way over to the bar, where he found a human spacer with a drink already in his hand. "Excuse me, my friend,"

Ben said, "but I wonder if I might have a word with you."

The spacer eyed Ben suspiciously and replied, "Well?"

Examining the design of the spacer's pressure suit, Ben continued, "You're a Corellian spacer, are you not?"

"What about it?"

"I'm in the market to charter a fast starship," Ben said, "and I've been told by those in the know that the Corellian vessels are among the very best."

"You heard right," the spacer replied. "'Cept that Corellians aren't *among*; we are the *best*."

"Ah, splendid," Ben said, beaming. "And would you by any chance know of a starship that's available for hire?"

The spacer's shoulders seemed to sag within his suit. "If you'd've come in here yesterday, you could've had mine, but now I'm committed to a charter. I raise ship tonight."

Ben grimaced. "A pity," he said. "Perhaps you could recommend someone else?"

"Well, there aren't too many other Corellians in port just now, and anybody else'd just be a second-rater." Scratching his chin while thinking, the spacer said, "Let's see, now . . . Oh, yeah, there's the *Falcon*."

"Falcon?"

"The *Millennium Falcon.* Her skipper's Han Solo."

"And would this — Han Solo? — be available at present for a job?"

"Haw!" the spacer laughed, nearly spilling his drink. "I'd be surprised if he wasn't. Han ain't been doing so well lately. He was around here a little while ago. In fact, his first mate, Chewbacca, he's . . ." The spacer glanced to his left and continued, "He's right here."

Ben followed the spacer's gaze to see a hulking, fur-covered alien who had moved up beside the bar. Chewbacca was a male Wookiee, about 2.25 meters tall. An ammunition bandolier was wrapped around the Wookiee's shaggy torso, and a laser-firing bowcaster was slung over one arm. Ben smiled and thought, *I haven't seen a Wookiee in a long time.*

Chewbacca nodded at Ben. The spacer stepped away from the bar so Ben could speak directly with the Wookiee.

Just then, Luke and C-3PO started down the steps from the lobby. A signal chimed behind them, and Ben heard the bartender bellow, "Hey, we don't serve their kind here!"

Luke replied, "What?"

"Your droids," the bartender said. "They'll have to wait outside. We don't want them here."

Ben watched as Luke dismissed C-3PO, who turned to exit the bar with R2-D2. Assured that no harm had occurred, Ben returned his attention to the Wookiee while Luke moved to stand beside him at the bar. Facing

Chewbacca, Ben said, "The *Millennium Falcon,* is that the name of your ship? I was told she's fast."

Chewbacca replied with a series of low barks and grunts. Fortunately, Ben understood enough of the Wookiee language to reply, "No, that will be more than satisfactory. I'm not looking for anything elaborate, Chewbacca, just quick passage to Alderaan —"

Before Ben could finish, Luke's right shoulder bumped into his side. He turned to see Luke face-to-face with a surly Aqualish, a tusked humanoid alien with bulbous black eyes. The Aqualish spat out combatively, "Negola dewaghi wooldugger?!?"

Luke looked away from the Aqualish, trying to ignore him. Ben watched as the Aqualish took a step back, allowing room for another thug to move in. Ben thought, *Oh, bother.*

The Aqualish's companion was a ghastly-looking man. The man's right eye was blinded and the flesh around it severely scarred. His nose looked as if it had an unfortunate encounter with a meat shredder. He tapped Luke's left shoulder — hard. Luke looked at the disfigured man, who gestured at the Aqualish before he leaned in close to Luke and snarled, "He doesn't like you."

Luke mumbled, "I'm sorry."

"I don't like you either," said the man. "You just watch yourself. We're wanted men. I have the death sentence on twelve systems."

Luke replied, "I'll be careful."

The man seized Luke's arm and snarled, "You'll be dead."

That's quite enough, Ben thought. Stepping away from Chewbacca, he moved behind Luke to face the disfigured man. Speaking calmly, Ben said, "This little one's not worth the effort. Come, let me get you something."

The disfigured man moved with alarming speed and strength, flinging Luke away from the bar. As Luke crashed into a nearby table, the man and the Aqualish reached for their blaster pistols.

"No blasters! No blasters!" the bartender shouted too late as he dropped behind the bar and the band stopped playing.

Ben's hand darted to his belt and he drew his lightsaber. The blade ignited and swept past the blaster-wielding criminals. The disfigured man fell back against the bar, a deep slash across his chest. The Aqualish screamed and his right arm — severed at the elbow — fell to the floor, still clutching the blaster.

Everyone in the cantina was silent. The entire fight was over in less than five seconds. The only sound to be heard was the hum of Ben's lightsaber. He stood his ground, holding his lightsaber out from his body as he stared at his two defeated opponents. Then he glanced out across the room. If anyone else had been looking for a fight, the look in Ben's eyes was enough to discourage them.

Ben deactivated his lightsaber. Almost immediately, the band started playing again, and the patrons went back to their drinks and conversations. It was business again as usual in the Mos Eisley cantina.

Chewbacca followed Ben over to Luke, who remained sprawled on the floor. As Ben reached down to help Luke up, Luke said, "I'm all right,"

Ben nodded at the Wookiee and said to Luke, "Chewbacca here is first mate on a ship that might suit us."

Chewbacca moved off to briefly confer with his captain, then guided Ben and Luke around the bar to a booth that had a circular table with a cylindrical light at its center. The booth was against the wall opposite the band, so they would be able to converse without shouting. The booth also offered a clear view of the entry lobby. Chewbacca sat with his back to the wall so he could watch the entry. Ben and Luke sat with their backs to the bar and faced Chewbacca.

They were soon joined by a tall, lean man with dark hair. The man wore a white shirt with a black vest, pants, and boots. As the man moved past the table, Ben noticed he had a blaster pistol in a quick-draw holster against his right thigh.

The man sat down beside Chewbacca, pointed to himself and said, "Han Solo. I'm captain of the

Millennium Falcon. Chewie here tells me you're looking for passage to the Alderaan system."

"Yes, indeed," Ben said. "If it's a fast ship."

"Fast ship?" Han said, sounding offended. "You've
never heard of the *Millennium Falcon*?"

Ben asked, "Should I have?"

"It's the ship that made the Kessel run in less than
twelve parsecs!"

Ben was not impressed with such obvious misinfor-
mation, and gave Han a look that said as much.

Han continued, "I've outrun Imperial starships, not
the local bulk cruisers, mind you. I'm talking about the
big Corellian ships now. She's fast enough for you, old
man. What's the cargo?"

"Only passengers," Ben said. "Myself, the boy, two
droids, and no questions asked."

Han grinned broadly. "What is it? Some kind of
local trouble?"

Ben said, "Let's just say we'd like to avoid any
Imperial entanglements."

Narrowing his gaze on Ben, Han said, "Well, that's
the real trick, isn't it? And it's going to cost you something extra." His eyes flicked to Luke. "Ten thousand,
all in advance."

"Ten thousand?" Luke gasped. "We could almost
buy our own ship for that!"

Han raised his eyebrows. "But who's going to fly it,
kid? You?"

"You bet I could," Luke said angrily. "I'm not such a bad pilot myself!" He looked to Ben and started to rise. "We don't have to sit here and listen —"

Ben touched Luke's arm, urging him to remain seated. Then Ben returned his gaze to Solo and said, "We can pay you two thousand now, plus fifteen when we reach Alderaan."

Han did the math. "Seventeen, huh?"

Ben nodded.

Han thought about the offer for a few seconds, keeping his steely eyes locked on Ben. "Okay," Han said. "You guys got yourselves a ship. We'll leave as soon as you're ready. Docking Bay Ninety-four."

"Ninety-four," Ben repeated.

Han looked past Ben to the bar and said, "Looks like somebody's beginning to take an interest in your handiwork."

Ben glanced at Luke, who turned to look at the bartender. Ben heard the bartender mutter something, then the stormtrooper's digitized voice replied, "All right, we'll check it out."

Facing Ben, Han said, "I suggest the backdoor, gents. Right over there." He tilted head slightly in the direction of the door.

By the time the stormtroopers arrived at Han and Chewbacca's table, Ben and Luke were gone. Outside the cantina, Ben raised his hood to cover his head as they walked fast for where they'd parked the landspeeder. C-3PO and R2-D2 stood beside the vehicle, waiting for them.

Ben considered Han's fee, then said to Luke, "You'll have to sell your speeder."

"That's okay," Luke said as they neared the droids. "I'm never coming back to this planet again."

INTERLUDE

"Tell me something, Artoo," Luke said as he worked on the components for his new lightsaber. "Did you ever think we'd wind up back on Tatooine again?"

The astromech droid was standing on the other side of the living area inside Ben's hut, and responded to Luke's question with a scathing beep. Then R2-D2 opened a slot beneath his domed head and loudly ejected some sand that had found its way into his cylindrical body.

"Yeah, that's how I feel, too," Luke replied. Although his life had changed dramatically in the past three years, and although he had a reason for returning to Tatooine, he still felt like something of a failure now, as if all his accomplishments had led him back to where he'd started from. He had sincerely believed on the day that he had left Tatooine on the Millennium Falcon with Ben that he would never set foot on the sand planet again.

In fact, after Luke had boarded the Millennium Falcon *with Ben and the droids, he hadn't been sure whether he would ever set foot on* any *planet again. First, a squad of stormtroopers had tried to stop the* Falcon *from leaving its docking bay at Mos Eisley, and then, as the* Falcon *raced away from Tatooine, it had drawn fire from a blockade of Imperial Star Destroyers. Fortunately, Han Solo had managed to evade and escape the blockade by launching the incredibly durable* Falcon *into hyperspace,*

But after the Falcon *emerged from hyperspace, Luke's group had immediately discovered that their destination, Alderaan, no longer existed. They were still pondering what could have caused the destruction of an entire planet when Solo began pursuit of a passing Imperial TIE fighter, which had led them directly toward a moon-sized battle station. Luke had been genuinely frightened when he first saw the Death Star. And when the* Falcon *was captured by the Death Star's tractor beam, he had thought that they were all goners.*

But Ben had remained calm as he quickly improvised a plan to infiltrate the battle station. He had instructed Han Solo to jettison some of the Falcon*'s escape pods and make an entry in the ship's log, claiming in the entry that the crew abandoned ship right after takeoff. Then Ben had instructed Luke, Han, Chewbacca, and the droids to hide within the ship's sensor-proofed* *concealed compartments, which Han had previously used for smuggling.*

After the tractor beam had deposited the Falcon *into a Death Star hangar, Han and Chewbacca subdued a scanning crew and two stormtroopers. Luke and Han had then disguised themselves in the fallen stormtroopers' armor, which allowed the group to sneak into a nearby control room. Once inside, R2-D2 had accessed a computer outlet to gain data on how to shut down power to the tractor beam and allow the* Falcon *to escape.*

Ben had insisted on going to the tractor-beam power coupling alone.

To this day, Luke wondered if Ben ever had any idea that he wouldn't be leaving the Death Star on the Millennium Falcon.

CHAPTER TWELVE

Inside the control room that overlooked Docking Bay 327, the hangar that held the captive *Millennium Falcon*, Ben rapidly studied the schematics for the power generator terminal that R2-D2 had displayed on a viewscreen. The terminal was located in sector six of the spherical battle station's northern hemisphere. Instantly memorizing the location, Ben turned to Luke and Han and said, "I don't think you boys can help. I must go alone."

"Whatever you say," Han replied as Ben headed for the door. "I've done more than I bargained for on this trip already."

Ben had just reached the door when he was stopped by Luke, who said, "I want to go with you."

"Be patient, Luke," Ben said. "Stay and watch over the droids."

Gesturing to Han, Luke said, "But he can —"

"They must be delivered safely or other star systems will suffer the same fate as Alderaan," Ben interrupted. "Your destiny lies along a different path from mine." He pressed a button on the doorway, and the door slid fast up into the ceiling. Facing Luke, he added, "The Force will be with you . . . always!"

Ben left the command office and moved down the corridor. A moment later, he heard the door slide shut behind him. Although he was reluctant to leave Luke alone with the brash Han Solo, he believed Luke would remain safe if he stayed where he was, at least until the tractor beam's power was deactivated.

He also believed it was best to put some distance between himself and Luke, because he knew something that the boy didn't. Shortly after they had arrived within the battle station's hangar, while still hiding within the *Falcon*'s smuggling compartment, Ben had sensed a most particular presence.

Darth Vader.

Ben knew that if he had sensed Vader, it was most likely that the Dark Lord had sensed him, too. Ben was not afraid of confronting Vader again, but he didn't even want to think about what would happen to Luke if he failed to shut down the tractor beam.

Ben was careful to avoid detection as he made his way through the battle station's maze of corridors and lift tubes. Moving stealthily from a lateral transport to a long, empty corridor, he clung to the shadows until he finally arrived at his destination: a narrow bridge that spanned a wide, deep shaft that delivered him to the tractor beam power terminal, a cylindrical structure that stood atop a thirty-five-kilometer-tall generator tower.

A narrow ledge wrapped around the terminal. Ben stepped carefully onto the ledge and moved around the power terminal until he could reach the generator controls. He pressed one lever, then edged further around the terminal until he found the controls for the tractor beam power coupling.

He heard footsteps approach. Ben maneuvered his body around the terminal to conceal himself from a detachment of stormtroopers as they crossed the shaft-spanning bridge. Two stormtroopers remained behind while the others proceeded.

After Ben readjusted the generator controls and confirmed that the tractor beam was disabled, he used the Force to make the two remaining stormtroopers think they heard a muffled explosion. While the stormtroopers were distracted, Ben stepped back onto the bridge, then moved quickly away from the terminal. He darted into another corridor, and began making his way back to the control room to rejoin his allies.

Ben eventually arrived at the battle station's equatorial area, and then to the same level as Docking Bay 327. He was moving through a corridor when he heard more stormtroopers approach, and he ducked into a dark alcove. As the stormtroopers passed his position, one trooper commented, "We think they may be splitting up. They may be on levels five and six now, sir."

Splitting up? Ben wasn't certain, but he suspected that the stormtrooper was referring to Luke and the others. All he could do was hope that Luke was all right.

Once the stormtroopers were gone, Ben emerged from the alcove and drew his lightsaber from his belt. He did not activate the blade but held it ready. He had a feeling he would be using his weapon sooner than later, and he had a feeling he would be using it against Vader.

Ever since he had first sensed Vader's presence on the battle station, he had become increasingly certain that Vader knew he was on board. He had even allowed the possibility that Vader had let him deactivate the tractor beam, all in an effort to lure him into a trap. Ben had no fear of whatever Vader might have in store for him, but he still had to do everything in his power to make sure Luke would escape safely.

If Ben failed that, he believed all his years on Tatooine would have been for nothing, and all *would* be lost.

He proceeded through the corridor, but with less caution. For now he knew he was destined to encounter Vader, and that it would be their final reunion.

Ben was still clutching his lightsaber when he reached an access tunnel that led back to Docking Bay

327. As he entered the tunnel, he sighted a tall, shadowy form at the tunnel's other the end. Even if Ben had never seen Darth Vader's cybernetic incarnation via a HoloNet broadcast on Tatooine, he still would have sensed the power of his former apprentice, now concealed within black armor.

Vader had already activated the red blade of his lightsaber. For a moment, he stood as still as a statue. Then he moved forward, his black cape sweeping behind him as he practically glided across the tunnel's floor toward Obi-Wan Kenobi.

Obi-Wan activated his lightsaber and stepped slowly forward. He'd fought Vader before, and he hadn't been afraid then, either. As Vader drew closer, Obi-Wan thought with morbid amusement, *He's taller than I remember.*

"I've been waiting for you, Obi-Wan," Vader said as he stepped even closer. "We meet again, at last. The circle is now complete."

Obi-Wan angled his lightsaber to assume an offensive position.

Vader continued, "When I left you, I was but the learner; now I am the master."

"Only a master of evil, Darth," Obi-Wan said. He used Vader's Sith Lord title mockingly, as if he were addressing an unfortunately named child. He had hoped the insult might catch Vader off guard, and followed with a sudden lunge, but Vader easily blocked it with his own weapon. There was a loud electric crackle as the blades made contact.

Obi-Wan swung again and again, and Vader parried each strike.

Vader said, "Your powers are weak, old man,"

Although Obi-Wan could only imagine what was left of Vader's features behind the black mask, he somehow suspected that Vader was smiling. "You can't win, Darth," Obi-Wan said. "If you strike me down, I shall become more powerful than you can possibly imagine."

"You should not have come back."

Their lightsabers clashed again and again. And as their battle continued, they moved closer to the main doorway that led directly to the *Millennium Falcon*'s hangar.

Obi-Wan risked a glance through the hangar's open doorway and saw four stormtroopers guarding the *Falcon.* He also sensed that Luke was nearby. Hoping to cause a distraction that would allow Luke to board the *Falcon,* he attacked Vader more vigorously. The noise of clashing lightsabers echoed into the hangar, attracting the stormtroopers' attention.

With his peripheral vision, Obi-Wan saw the stormtroopers leave their stations beside the *Falcon* and run toward him and Vader. He continued his attack on Vader, and several exchanges later, he sensed Luke's movement and knew his plan had worked. He risked another glance into the hangar to see several figures racing for the *Falcon*'s landing ramp: the droids, Chewbacca, Han Solo, Luke, and — *Leia*!

Obi-Wan hadn't known that Princess Leia was on the battle station, but he recognized the girl in the white dress from the hologram that R2-D2 had displayed. Obi-Wan did not believe in luck or coincidences, and seeing Luke unwittingly reunited with his twin sister, he knew that it was not a tractor beam that had brought him to the battle station, but the will of the Force.

His fleeting glance also registered that Luke had paused behind his friends. Luke stood a short distance from the landing ramp and was staring straight at him, gaping.

Obi-Wan realized there was only one way Luke, Leia, and the others would escape the battle station alive. He smiled as he looked away from Luke, then closed his eyes and raised his lightsaber up before him.

Darth Vader did not hesitate to strike.

INTERLUDE

Luke Skywalker recalled the last moment he saw Ben alive, fighting Darth Vader on the Death Star. Ben had glanced at him from across the hangar, and then closed his eyes as he turned to face Vader. Vader's lightsaber cut right through Ben's robes, Ben's body had vanished . . .

And then he told me to run!

Luke didn't know if he would ever completely understand the Force, but he was relieved to know that somehow, it had kept Ben alive. Ben's voice — his spirit — had aided Luke when he'd flown his X-wing starfighter on the mission to destroy the Death Star. Without Ben's help, Luke doubted he ever could have accomplished that.

Luke had not yet finished reading Ben's journal, and wondered if he'd find anything in it about Jedi spirits. Do all Jedi become spirits like Ben? Or was it something Ben learned how to do on his own? *Luke had no idea.*

And again, he found himself wishing Ben were there to answer his questions.

CHAPTER THIRTEEN

Thanks to the teachings of Qui-Gon Jinn, Obi-Wan Kenobi was one with the Force.

Where he had been once but an isolated drop of water in a great sea, he was now the sea itself. It was a sea that had no surface or floor, which flowed everywhere and through everything. The Force transcended time and space. Civilizations would rise and fall, stars would form and die, but the Force would never end.

As a spiritual entity, Obi-Wan was not hampered by the laws of physics. He could travel across the galaxy from one world to another by merely thinking of the journey. He could not only communicate with the living but manifest an illusion of his former physical self. He could even communicate with fellow spirits, should they be mutually inclined.

After the destruction of the Death Star, Obi-Wan limited his communication with Luke Skywalker. This was not because Obi-Wan's powers would have been in any way diminished by further communication, but because he knew that there were a great many things that Luke could learn only from the living — not only his friends but his enemies as well. More precisely, there were things Luke had to learn for himself, and sometimes on his own. Ben was a *guiding* spirit, not a meddling one.

But Obi-Wan's spirit always remained watchful. After Luke accidentally became catatonic while attempting to use the Force to meditate, Obi-Wan entered Luke's dreams and guided him to conquer his innate fear of Darth Vader. And when the very unprepared Luke and Leia — still unaware of the fact that they were siblings — actually confronted Vader on Mimban, Obi-Wan again intervened, bolstering Luke's abilities to help him defeat the Dark Lord.

Vader should have died on Mimban, Obi-Wan thought ruefully. *Just as he should have died on Mustafar, Yavin, and more places than I can name.*

And yet Darth Vader lived.

As powerful as Obi-Wan was in spirit, he had no influence over the Sith Lords. In fact, to be anywhere near their proximity was a draining experience for any entity.

And there were other dangers to consider. Yoda had told him that ancient Sith Lords had at least once developed a weapon called the Thought Bomb to destroy Jedi and capture their souls. Obi-Wan did not know whether

Palpatine or Vader possessed or were capable of creating a Thought Bomb or if such a weapon could consume an already existing spirit, but he knew that if he allowed himself to be lured into any Sith-set trap, he would be of little use to Luke.

It was three years after the Battle of Yavin, when the Rebel Alliance had relocated to the ice planet Hoth, that Ben manifested himself as a vision to Luke. Luke had escaped the clutches of a bloodthirsty wampa on his own, but he was also injured and lost, far from the Rebel base. Exhausted by his struggle to survive and by the sub-freezing winds that tore at him from all directions, Luke collapsed against the hard, snow-covered ground.

Obi-Wan spoke. "Luke . . . Luke."

Slowly, Luke raised his head as if it were a massive weight. Obi-Wan appeared as a shimmering, spectral form a short distance in front of him. Obi-Wan could see in Luke's confused expression that he was wondering whether he was hallucinating. Luke said aloud, "Ben?"

Ben said, "You will go to the Dagobah system."

"Dagobah system?" Luke repeated, still confused.

"There you will learn from Yoda," Obi-Wan continued, "the Jedi Master who instructed me."

Luke groaned. "Ben . . . Ben."

Obi-Wan knew that Luke was in shock. But he also knew that help would arrive within seconds, in the form of Han Solo riding a tauntaun. Han Solo would believe that he had arrived upon Luke's position by pure luck, but it was Obi-Wan who had steered Han's mount to the north of the wampa's ice cave.

Obi-Wan dematerialized just a moment before Han arrived upon Luke.

Obi-Wan's spirit monitored Luke's recovery in the bacta tank at the Rebel base, and through the terrible battle at Hoth. When the Rebels were forced to evacuate, he watched Luke's progress. He did not intervene when Luke crash-landed his X-wing into the Dagobah swamp — Obi-Wan did not want Luke to leave before his training was complete.

Obi-Wan was a secret witness to the moment Luke unknowingly met Yoda, who was reluctant to introduce himself until he was convinced of Luke's conviction to study the ways of the Jedi. Obi-Wan even watched with some amusement as Yoda offered to take Luke to meet "the Jedi Master" he sought, only to bring Luke to his own low-ceilinged hut under the large roots of an ancient tree.

Addressing Luke as he prepared some food in a steaming pot, Yoda said, "Why wish you become Jedi? Hm?"

"Mostly because of my father, I guess," Luke replied.

"Ah, father," Yoda said with interest. "Powerful Jedi was he, mmm, powerful Jedi, mmm."

"Oh, come on!" Luke said angrily. "How could you know my father? You don't even know who I am. Oh, I don't know what I'm doing here. We're wasting our time."

Yoda looked away from Luke and leaned his weight onto the gimer stick that he used as a walking staff. Obi-Wan sensed the aged Jedi Master's disappointment even before he said, "I cannot teach him. The boy has no patience."

"He will learn patience," Obi-Wan said aloud, his voice echoing slightly within the hut.

Startled by the disembodied voice, Luke glanced around the hut, searching for Obi-Wan.

"Hmmm," muttered Yoda. He turned slowly to face Luke. Speaking to Obi-Wan, he said, "Much anger in him, like his father."

Obi-Wan's voice replied, "Was I any different when you taught me?"

"Hah," Yoda said. "He is not ready."

Luke finally stopped looking for Obi-Wan and looked into his host's wise old eyes. Luke gasped, "Yoda!"

Yoda nodded.

"I *am* ready," Luke protested. "I . . . Ben! I . . . I can be a Jedi. Ben, tell him I'm ready." Luke started to get up, only to smack his head in the hut's ceiling.

"Ready, are you?" Yoda said with disdain. "What know you of ready? For eight hundred years have I trained Jedi. My own counsel will I keep on who is to be trained! A Jedi must have the deepest commitment, the most serious mind." Tilting his head back to address the invisible Obi-Wan, Yoda continued, "This one a long time have I watched. All his life has he looked away . . . to the future, to the horizon. Never his mind on where he was. Hmm? What he was doing. Hmph." He raised his gimer stick and jabbed Luke. "Adventure. Heh! Excitement. Heh! A Jedi craves not these things." Then he lowered his gimer stick, glared at Luke and said, "You are reckless!"

Obi-Wan said, "So was I, if you remember."

"He is too old," Yoda said firmly. "Yes, too old to begin training."

Luke said desperately, "But I've learned so much."

Yoda sighed. Again addressing Obi-Wan's spirit, he asked, "Will he finish what he begins?"

Luke did not wait for Obi-Wan's answer, and said, "I won't fail you."

Yoda returned his gaze to Luke, who added, "I'm not afraid."

"Oh," Yoda said, his eyes widening slightly. Lowering his voice to a threatening tone, he said, "You will be. You *will* be."

Luke's training was brutal. Not just the obstacle courses that had him climbing vines and leaping through the swamp with Yoda secured to his back, but also the meditation exercises to open himself to the Force. Luke obeyed Yoda's every instruction and never broke down.

Obi-Wan's spirit silently watched Luke's progress as the young man tackled every challenge. *Every day, he's getting stronger,* Obi-Wan thought.

Still, Luke was limited by his self-doubts, and his impulse to confront danger. He had entered a cave that was inexplicably strong with the dark side of the Force, only to have a nightmarish confrontation with an apparition of Darth Vader. He had refused to believe the Force could be used to elevate his sinking X-wing until Yoda showed him that it *was* possible. Even more crippling were his fears, especially after meditation had yielded a vision of the future, of a city in the clouds, where his friends Leia and Han would meet with pain.

"I've got to go to them," Luke said.

Yoda sighed. "Decide you must how to serve them best. If you leave now, help them you could. But you would destroy all for which they have fought and suffered."

And yet Luke decided to leave Dagobah. As darkness fell, Luke put on his orange flight suit and checked his gear while R2-D2 positioned himself into the X-wing's astromech socket.

"Luke!" said Yoda, watching from a nearby knoll. "You must complete the training."

"I can't keep the vision out of my head," Luke replied as he hastily inspected his ship. "They're my friends. I've got to help them."

"You must not go!" Yoda said desperately.

Luke faced Yoda and said, "But Han and Leia will die if I don't."

"You don't know that," replied the disembodied voice of Obi-Wan's spirit. *If Yoda can't convince Luke to stay, perhaps I can.*

Turning in response to Obi-Wan's voice, Luke watched as a slightly shimmering light began to glow in the air behind Yoda. Then the light materialized into the form of Obi-Wan, who said gravely, "Even Yoda cannot see their fate."

"But I can help them!" Luke said. "I feel the Force!"

"But you cannot control it," Obi-Wan said. "This is a dangerous time for you, when you will be tempted by the dark side of the Force."

Yoda said, "Yes, yes. To Obi-Wan you listen. The cave. Remember your failure at the cave!"

"But I've learned so much since then, Master Yoda," Luke said as he returned his attention to his X-wing. "I promise to return and finish what I've begun. You have my word."

Obi-Wan said, "It is you and your abilities the Emperor wants. That is why your friends are made to suffer."

"That's why I have to go," Luke said.

"Luke," Obi-Wan said, "I don't want to lose you to the Emperor the way I lost Vader." To himself, Obi-Wan added, *The way I lost Anakin.*

"You won't," Luke said.

Yoda said, "Stopped they must be. On this all depends. Only a fully trained Jedi Knight with the Force as his ally will conquer Vader and his Emperor." As Luke stowed the last of his gear onto the X-wing, Yoda continued, "If you end your training now, if you choose the quick and easy path, as Vader did, you will become an agent of evil."

"Patience," Obi-Wan said with emphasis, hoping Luke would carry the word with him.

"And sacrifice Han and Leia?" Luke snapped. He was anything but patient.

Yoda answered, "If you honor what they fight for . . . yes!"

Luke reached for the lower rung of the X-wing's retractable ladder and looked away from Obi-Wan and Yoda. Obi-Wan said, "If you choose to face Vader, you will do it alone. I cannot interfere."

"I understand," Luke muttered. Then he climbed the ladder to the starfighter's open cockpit and said, "Artoo, fire up the converters."

As the X-Wing's engines fired up, Obi-Wan said, "Luke, don't give in to hate — that leads to the dark side."

"Strong is Vader," Yoda added. "Mind what you have learned. Save you it can."

"I will," Luke said as he pulled on his helmet. "And I'll return. I promise." The cockpit canopy lowered, and the X-wing lifted off from the ground and ascended into the night sky.

As Yoda raised his gaze to watch the departing X-Wing, Obi-Wan's luminous apparition faded into the darkness. Yoda sighed, looked down at the ground, and shook his head sadly. "Told you, I did," he said. "Reckless is he. Now matters are worse."

Obi-Wan's disembodied voice said, "That boy is our last hope."

Yoda returned his gaze to the sky and said, "No. There is another."

Obi-Wan knew Yoda was speaking of Luke's sister, Leia. Although Leia shared Luke's bloodline and was certainly strong-willed, and although Obi-Wan had always respected Yoda's beliefs, he somehow remained convinced that only one person could defeat the Sith Lords, and that person was Luke.

CHAPTER FOURTEEN

Luke Skywalker made the final adjustments to his new lightsaber. He was sitting at the table in the living area of Ben Kenobi's hut on Tatooine. Ben's journal rested on the table, its pages opened to the section on lightsabers. R2-D2 stood across the room, silently watching Luke.

I wish Ben were here, Luke thought absently, and not just because he had questions about Darth Vader. Sometimes, he just missed Ben.

Ben's spirit had not communicated with him since Dagobah, which did not surprise Luke. After all, Luke had ignored Ben and Yoda's cautions, and had gone directly to the Bespin system, and straight into Darth Vader's trap.

Ben had been good to his word. When Luke chose to face Darth Vader, Ben's spirit had done nothing to interfere. In hindsight, Luke realized that Ben and Yoda were right, that he should have stayed on Dagobah, for he accomplished very little by going to Cloud City.

I didn't stop Boba Fett from taking Han. I only endangered Leia and the others when they circled back to Cloud City to get me. I didn't rescue any of my friends. They rescued me!

And what did I accomplish? All he could think of was his confrontation with Vader, not just that he had survived the duel but that he had gained some information. As for the value of that devastating information . . .

Is Vader really my father?

Again, Luke felt the phantom pain at his right wrist.

R2-D2 saw Luke staring blankly at nothing in particular, and the droid chirped in concern.

Luke looked up at R2-D2 and said, "Don't worry, I'm fine." Returning his attention to the lightsaber, he added, "Well, I guess I'd better test it." He got up, carrying the lightsaber as he headed for the door. The astromech droid followed him outside.

It was early evening, with only a few stars visible in the sky. Luke held the lightsaber in his right hand. He was nervous. Even though he had followed Ben's instructions to the letter, and had checked and re-checked every part of the lightsaber during its construction, he still allowed the possibility that the weapon might explode. It was this uncertainty that had prompted him to test the weapon outside. If it *did* explode, he didn't want to destroy Ben's house along with it.

Watching Luke, R2-D2 beeped anxiously, and then extended a manipulator arm in his direction.

"You're offering to test my lightsaber?"

R2-D2 whistled affirmatively.

"Thanks, Artoo, but I wouldn't be much of a Jedi if I let you or anyone else do that."

R2-D2 retracted his manipulator and trembled, kicking up dirt.

"Go back inside," Luke ordered.

R2-D2 protested with a loud, blurting noise.

"Go on," Luke said. "If something happens, I need you to tell Leia." Luke thought, *Yeah. Tell her Luke, the galaxy's biggest idiot, flash-flamed himself into a black crisp because he couldn't follow an elementary circuit diagram.*

R2-D2 stomped off back to the house, protesting all the way.

Luke relaxed and let his breath out. He waited until R2 had entered the house, then took another deep breath, held it, and pressed the lightsaber's activation plate.

VMMMMM — !

The lightsaber's gleaming green blade extended to its full length, just under a meter. Luke moved it back and forth through the air, listening to it hum.

Luke released his held breath. He hadn't *really* expected the lightsaber to explode, but was still relieved that it hadn't. The weapon felt comfortable in his hand, even better balanced than his previous lightsaber.

But will it cut? Luke walked over to a thin spire of rock that jutted up from the dry ground. He swept the blade down at an angle through the top of the rock. He felt no resistance as the blade traveled through the rock, but there was a loud crack as the rock separated and the top piece slid down the smooth surface of the angled cut.

Holding the lightsaber, Luke felt grateful to Ben for having left his journal behind. *I never would have gotten this far without Ben,* Luke thought. And then, because he had learned that lightsaber construction was a rite of passage for a Jedi, he wondered, *Am I a Jedi now?*

Luke was unaware that Obi-Wan's spirit, even now, could hear his thoughts.

Obi-Wan's spirit knew that Luke had to complete one final task before he could call himself a Jedi.

Liberating Han Solo from Jabba the Hutt wasn't easy, but Luke Skywalker and his allies pulled it off. Part of their daring rescue plan had included R2-D2 smuggling Luke's new lightsaber into Jabba's palace and delivering it to Luke when a signal was given. The plan had worked extremely well.

Immediately after the rescue, Luke returned with R2-D2 to Dagobah. Luke had hoped to resume his training with Yoda, but by the time they arrived on the swamp world, the aged Jedi Master was close to death.

Luke was with Yoda when he died. Night had fallen, and Yoda had been lying under blankets on his small bed when he breathed his last. Just seconds later, Luke watched as Yoda's body dematerialized and vanished. After 900 years, Yoda had finally become one with the Force.

But moments before he died, Yoda confirmed the truth about Darth Vader. Vader *was* Luke's father, and only by confronting him again could Luke become a Jedi. Yoda also disclosed that there existed another Skywalker.

Leaving Yoda's hut, Luke stepped out into the darkness and readied his X-wing to leave Dagobah. But then he looked to R2-D2 and said, "I can't do it, Artoo. I can't go on alone."

It was then that Obi-Wan chose to speak: "Yoda will always be with you."

Luke turned. "Obi-Wan!"

Obi-Wan's shimmering apparition materialized before a nearby grove of trees. He moved away from the trees to stand facing Luke.

Advancing toward Obi-Wan's spirit, Luke said, "Why didn't you tell me? You told me Vader betrayed and murdered my father."

"Your father was seduced by the dark side of the Force," Obi-Wan replied. "He ceased to be Anakin Skywalker and became Darth Vader. When that happened, the good man who was your father was destroyed. So what I told you was true . . . from a certain point of view."

"A certain point of view?" Luke echoed. The look on his face made it clear to Obi-Wan that he found the words distasteful.

"Luke, you're going to find that many of the truths we cling to depend greatly on our own point of view." Obi-Wan shifted his apparition, easing himself to sit on the moss-covered trunk of a fallen tree. "Anakin was a good friend."

Luke sat down beside Obi-Wan's apparition. Obi-Wan continued, "When I first knew him, your father was already a great pilot. But I was amazed how strongly the Force was with him. I took it upon myself to train him as a Jedi. I thought that I could instruct him just as well as Yoda. I was wrong."

"There is still good in him," Luke said.

Unconvinced, Obi-Wan said dismissively, "He's more machine now than man. Twisted and evil."

Luke shook his head. "I can't do it, Ben."

"You cannot escape your destiny. You must face Darth Vader again."

"I can't kill my own father."

Obi-Wan looked away from Luke. "Then the

Emperor has already won," he said with a sigh. "You were our only hope."

"Yoda spoke of another."

Obi-Wan returned his gaze to Luke. "The other he spoke of is your twin sister."

Luke looked baffled. "But I have no sister."

"To protect you both from the Emperor, you were hidden from your father when you were born. The Emperor knew, as I did, if Anakin were to have any offspring, they would be a threat to him. That is the reason why your sister remains safely anonymous."

Luke's eyes went wide with realization. "Leia!" he said. "Leia's my sister."

"Your insight serves you well," Obi-Wan said. Making sure Luke had his complete attention, Obi-Wan continued, "Bury your feelings deep down, Luke. They do you credit. But they could be made to serve the Emperor."

Luke nodded in agreement.

And then Obi-Wan vanished into the darkness.

Obi-Wan's spirit was invisible but present when Luke arrived in the Endor system, where the Empire had constructed a new Death Star battle station. When Luke surrendered to Darth Vader on the Endor forest moon, he listened as Luke maintained his belief that a remnant of Anakin Skywalker remained within Vader and had not been entirely consumed by evil. Luke urged his father to let go of his hate.

Vader said, "It is too late for me, son." Then he signaled to two stormtroopers to escort Luke to a waiting shuttle that would carry them to the Death Star. As the stormtroopers moved up behind Luke, Vader added, "The Emperor will show you the true nature of the Force. He is your Master now."

Luke stared at Vader for a moment before he said, "Then my father is truly dead."

Obi-Wan's spirit wished he had convinced Luke of this fact earlier.

After Vader delivered Luke to the Emperor's throne room on the Death Star, and the black-cloaked Emperor orchestrated a lightsaber duel to test father against son, Obi-Wan became even more resolved that Luke had been unprepared for the confrontation. *He's afraid of what will happen to Leia if he fails to defeat Vader*, Obi-Wan thought. *He* must *kill Vader.*

But when Luke finally managed to disarm and subdue Vader, Obi-Wan's spirit practically cringed when the Emperor fixed his yellow eyes on Luke and said, "Good! Your hate has made you powerful. Now, fulfill your destiny and take your father's place at my side!"

Obi-Wan feared that he would lose Luke as he had Anakin. But then Luke deactivated his lightsaber, faced the Emperor, and said, "Never!" He flung his lightsaber aside. "I'll never turn to the dark side. You've failed, Your Highness. I am a Jedi, like my father before me."

The Emperor scowled. "So be it . . . *Jedi*."

And then the Emperor raised his gnarled fingers and unleashed his wrath on Luke, launching bolts of blue lightning at him. Luke screamed and writhed in agony, and then the Emperor released another barrage.

Vader was lying near the throne room's elevator shaft, where he'd collapsed during his duel with Luke. While the Emperor continued his assault on Luke, Obi-Wan's spirit monitored Vader as the injured figure staggered to his feet and returned to the Emperor's side.

"Father, please," Luke groaned. "Help me."

Obi-Wan knew that Vader would never help, and he felt almost overwhelmed by a sense of dread. Luke would soon be dead, and Vader would remain the Emperor's puppet. In fact, Obi-Wan was so convinced of Vader's nature that he was stunned by what happened next.

Vader grabbed the Emperor and lifted him off his feet. The deadly blue lightning fell away from Luke and arced back from the Emperor's fingertips and crashed down upon the Sith Lords. Vader carried the Emperor across the throne room and hurled him down into the elevator shaft. A moment later, the Emperor exploded in a great release of dark energy.

Vader collapsed near the edge of the elevator shaft. Luke went to his side and eased his armored body to the floor. A thin, wheezing noise hissed from the ventilator on Vader's mask. His breathing apparatus was damaged.

Had Obi-Wan's spirit not witnessed Vader's action, he never would have believed it. Vader, the same monster that Obi-Wan had left to die on Mustafar, had sacrificed himself to save his son. And suddenly Obi-Wan realized where he had failed. For unlike Luke, Obi-Wan had not only believed that Anakin was completely consumed by the dark side, but had actually *refused* to believe that any goodness could have remained within Vader. And by refusing to allow that possibility, Obi-Wan had condemned not only his former friend but his own capacity for hope.

Fortunately, Luke's unwavering faith in his father's innate goodness had proved to be a stronger force than the power of the dark side.

Obi-Wan recalled what Qui-Gon Jinn's spirit had told him so long ago, when he said that Obi-Wan was not ready, and that he failed to understand. For so many years, Obi-Wan had thought Qui-Gon meant that he wasn't ready to comprehend details about Anakin's conversion to the dark side. But now, he finally understood his Master's words.

I wasn't ready to forgive Anakin. And he won't be entirely free unless I do.

Unfortunately, just as Obi-Wan realized that Anakin Skywalker lived, he also knew that Anakin would not live much longer. As Luke hauled his dying father toward a shuttle, Obi-Wan's spirit shifted his own psyche to another realm. And he waited.

After Anakin died in his son's arms, Obi-Wan called out into the void, "Anakin."

A moment later, Obi-Wan heard a familiar voice return from the darkness. "Obi-Wan? Master, I'm so sorry. So very, very —"

"Anakin, listen carefully," Obi-Wan interrupted. "You are in the netherworld of the Force, but if you ever wish to revisit corporeal space, then I still have one thing left to teach you. A way to become one with the Force. If you choose this path to immortality, then you must listen now, before your consciousness fades."

Obi-Wan sensed confusion and remorse in Anakin's psyche, then Anakin answered, "But Master . . . why me?"

"Because you ended the horror, Anakin," Obi-Wan said. "Because you fulfilled the prophecy. Because you were . . . and are . . . the Chosen One."

But Obi-Wan knew in his heart that those were not the only reasons. He added, "Because I was wrong about you. And because I am your friend."

Anakin answered quietly, "Thank you, Master."

Luke Skywalker managed to haul his father's body into an Imperial shuttle and escaped the Death Star before his Rebel Alliance allies destroyed the battle station. After landing on the forest moon, he gathered deadwood to build a funeral pyre to cremate Anakin's armored remains. As he watched the flames rise into the night sky, he wished he had somehow been able to help his father sooner.

When the pyre burned no more, Luke rejoined his friends. The Rebels were having a victory celebration with their new allies, the diminutive fur-covered Ewoks, at the Ewoks' treetop village. Shortly after Luke arrived, he looked away from his jubilant friends to see the spectral, luminescent forms of Obi-Wan and Yoda appear nearby, against the darkness of the forest canopy. A moment later, a third spirit appeared beside the others. It was Anakin Skywalker.

The Jedi had returned.

EPILOGUE

Obi-Wan Kenobi saw Luke Skywalker standing a short distance from the entry dome of the Lars family homestead on Tatooine. The twin suns were closing in on the horizon and cast long shadows across the desert. Luke was facing the sunset, his back to Obi-Wan. A warm, gentle wind was blowing in from the west.

But neither Obi-Wan nor Luke was really on Tatooine.

It was five years after the Battle of Endor. Luke Skywalker was in his modest apartment at the former Imperial Palace on Coruscant, where he had reluctantly taken up residence after the Rebel Alliance defeated the Empire and formed the New Republic. Lying on his bed, he was sound asleep, and dreaming of Tatooine.

Obi-Wan said, "Luke?"

Luke turned away from the suns. "Hello, Ben," he said with a welcoming smile. "Been a long time."

"It has indeed," Obi-Wan replied. "And I'm afraid that it will be longer still until next time. I've come to say good-bye, Luke."

The desert landscape and the sky itself seemed to shimmer and shudder, and Obi-Wan realized that Luke was now suddenly aware of the fact that he was dreaming. Luke's smile melted, and he looked at Obi-Wan cautiously.

Sensing Luke's thoughts, Obi-Wan said, "No, I'm not a dream. But the distances separating us have become too great for me to appear to you in any other way." He gestured at the surrounding dreamscape and added, "Now, even this last path is being closed to me."

"No," Luke said. "You can't leave us, Ben. We need you."

"You don't need me, Luke," Obi-Wan said, lifting his eyebrows slightly as he smiled. "You are a Jedi." Then his smile faded. "At any rate, the decision is not mine to make. I have lingered too long already, and can no longer postpone my journey from this life to what lies beyond."

Luke looked away from Obi-Wan, who sensed the young man's thoughts had turned to Yoda. Despite all that Luke had learned about the Force, he remained deeply saddened by the deaths of his friends.

"It is the pattern of all life to move on," Obi-Wan said. "You, too, will face this journey one day. You are strong in the Force, Luke, and with perseverance and discipline you will grow stronger still." Obi-Wan's gaze hardened as he added, "But you must never relax your guard. The Emperor is gone, but the dark side is still powerful. Never forget that."

"I won't."

"You will yet face great dangers, Luke." Then Obi-Wan's expression softened, and his smile returned as he continued, "But you will also find new allies at times and places where you expect them least."

"New allies?" Luke said, genuinely curious. "Who are they?"

Knowing that it was best not to reveal everything to Luke, Obi-Wan chose to ignore the question. As he felt himself begin to slip away from Luke's dream, he said, "And now, farewell. I loved you as a son, and as a student, and as a friend. Until we meet again, may the Force be with you."

"Ben — !"

Obi-Wan's form had vanished, but his psyche lingered long enough to sense Luke think to himself, *Then I am alone. I am the last of the Jedi.*

"Not the last of the old Jedi, Luke," Obi-Wan said, his voice trailing off across the dimension of dreams. "The first of the new."

And Obi-Wan finally moved on.

ABOUT THE AUTHOR

Ryder Windham's many books for Scholastic include *Star Wars: The Rise and Fall of Darth Vader* and junior novelizations of the *Star Wars Trilogy, Indiana Jones and the Raiders of the Lost Ark*, and *Indiana Jones and the Last Crusade*. He is also the author of *Star Wars: The Ultimate Visual Guide* (DK) and *Star Wars: Jedi vs. Sith: The Essential Guide to the Force* (Del Rey). He lives in Providence, Rhode Island, with his family.